SAM RAZOR - PRIVATE INVESTIGATOR

THE CASE

OF THE

BLONDE

WITH THE

BAD NOSE JOB

SAM RAZOR - PRIVATE INVESTIGATOR

THE CASE

OF THE

BLONDE

WITH THE

BAD NOSE JOB

CARLO ARMENISE

NEXT CENTURY
PUBLISHING

The Case of the Blonde with the Bad Nose Job
A Sam Razor Private Investigator Story

Published by Next Century Publishing
Austin, Texas
www.NextCenturyPublishing.com

ISBN: 978-1-68102-885-9

Printed in the United States of America

THE CASE

OF THE

BLONDE

WITH THE

BAD NOSE JOB

CHAPTER ONE

THE SET-UP

Here I am, another night in my car trying to catch one somebody doing something they're not supposed to be doing, with another somebody they're not supposed to do it with. That's what private investigators do, or at least it's what this private investigator does. Name's Sam Razor, and in the spirit of full disclosure my real last name isn't Razor, it's Lungelo. I use the DBA Razor for marketing purposes. I mean come on, Sam Razor, you got to love it. And in this business, it's important to have a catchy name people remember, like Sam Spade or Mickey Spillane, and Sam Razor's one of those.

Why does someone become a private investigator? Well, I can't speak for anyone else, but I did it for two reasons. First, because I come from a long line of P.I.s; my dad was a P.I., my grandfather was a P.I. and my great grandfather was just a cheater caught by a P.I. Second, I did it because of some advice I got from my dad when I was growing up. He told me no matter what I did for a living, make sure I was the "fuckor" and not the "fuckee." To do that he recommended becoming a lawyer, politician, or private investigator. He included private investigators because they either had something on somebody they'd have to pay to keep quiet, or could dig up something they'd want to pay to keep quiet, in other words, a recession proof business that didn't require a lot of education and only a small amount of ambition; two of the qualities I have in spades. I went the private investigator route because I couldn't lie well enough to be a politician and had too much conscience to be a lawyer, and besides, my dad was already in the business and helped me cut through the regulations and red tape and gave me my first job. In the beginning, working with my dad was fine, even though we didn't agree on much of anything when it came to cases. But after ten years, our disagreements became so confrontational, I decided to go off on my own. And when I did, my dad took it so hard he had a heart attack and died. And even though the autopsy showed four of his arteries were clogged and he didn't know it, I still blamed myself for his death, and decided the right thing to do was take over the agency and keep his legacy alive. It's nice when you can inherit a business that's doing well, but unfortunately the agency wasn't doing well; my dad had mismanaged the finances so badly it was on the verge of bankruptcy. I miss you, Dad.

While I'm not using my real last name, I didn't touch my family heritage, in fact, I verified it. I paid a boatload of money to one of those ancestor sites, and found out I'm seventy-five percent Italian on my dad's side of the family, and twenty-four percent Mexican on my mother's side. And one-percent Chinese, but we won't go into that. For the record, my mother's not an illegal, sneak across the border in the back of a pick-up truck Mexican, she's the daughter of one of the wealthiest land developers in Mexico City. Rumor had it my grandfather's main source of income wasn't land development, it was "pot development," but my brother and I couldn't talk about that growing up because my mother wouldn't admit it. When we asked what our grandfather did for a living, she told us he grew and sold vegetables to poor third world countries. We knew that wasn't true, unless they figured out a way to make pot look like tomatoes. But out of love for our mom, we kept our opinions to ourselves, and visited our grandfather every chance we got.

My parents met when my dad was doing some investigative work for my grandfather. He was being blackmailed and hired my dad to find out who it was. But according to my mom all he investigated was her, and six months later they got married. And over the next forty years they had two sons, two grandchildren, and a happy life. Thank God. Oh, I forgot to mention, we're Catholic. All Italian/Mexicans are, it's in our DNA.

I'm the younger half of the two sons and my brother Pepe is the older half. Pepe was named after my mother's father, Pepe Luigi Lungelo, and I was named after my dad's, Sam Jesus Lungelo. It's funny, the most vulnerable time of our lives is when we're born, and our parents take that opportunity to stick us with a name they like, without our permission or our participation. That's how we end up with names like Tailpipe and Autumn Breeze, so I guess I was lucky to get the name Sam, better than Tailpipe.

My brother's an investigator, too, but not the private kind, he's a Sargent for the CSI division of the local Police Department. Pepe's the best investigator in the division, or at least that's what he tells me every chance he gets; what he lacks in skill, he makes up in ego. We don't see each other very often because he's married with a couple of kids, and I'm divorced with a bird. It's not mine, it was my ex-wife's; she dumped it on me when she ran off with my best friend. For some unknown reason, she loved birds and thought they were the best pets you could have. They didn't have to be walked, didn't hump your leg, and didn't scratch the furniture, all they did was eat, sleep and shit in their cage. She named this current parrot Rainbow because of its multicolored feathers, and I renamed it "Shut the Fuck Up," because it won't shut the fuck up and repeats everything it hears, which means its vocabulary is mostly cusswords.

My brother and I aren't close. He's the straitlaced, "play by the book" type and I'm the "crooked laces, forget the book" type. And even though we disagree on just about everything, we still love each other and get together for holidays, birthdays, and personal time with mom, when I can get someone to watch Shut the Fuck Up.

Anyway, now that you know a little about my background, let me tell you about the case I just finished. The client was a super rich advertising executive who thought his wife was having an affair and hired me to find out. All my clients, both men and women, suspect their spouses of cheating, that's why they hire me, and most of the time they're right. In my experience, men cheat and get caught more than women, but when women do get caught, they blame the man, and get the house and everything in it. That's what happened in my divorce. As I said earlier, my wife was cheating on me with my best friend. He and I became friends in high school and did everything together, including joining the football team. He was the starting quarterback and captain of the team, and I was captain of the Gatorade. And while he was popular with all the girls, I had only one girlfriend, and she turned out to be the girl I married. While we stayed in contact and remained friends throughout our lives, we went in different directions when it came to our careers. He didn't go to college, even though he got a few football scholarships, and instead pursued a life of crime, which meant he was always in jail. Meanwhile, I did go to college, became a P.I. and spent my life staying away from jails. He had just been released from his latest stretch and needed a place to stay, so I let him move in with my wife and me. I know, it sounds more stupid every time I say it, but we were such good friends I didn't think he'd ever screw me over. But one afternoon, about a month into his stay, I came home from work and caught him in bed with my wife, doing something that looked like sex. I wasn't sure, because my wife and I hadn't had sex in so long, it looked to me like they were just wrestling, naked. I guess he figured that since I let him move in with us, it gave him permission to share everything in the house, including my wife. And even though she was the one who cheated, she claimed it was my fault because I spent too much time working and ignoring her. Her lawyer called it irreconcilable differences; I called it having a job. The court sided with her and gave her the house and a shit-load of alimony, and I got "Shut the Fuck Up." So in the end she was right, she said she slept with my friend because we had irreconcilable differences, and so now we do.

The cheating wife in the case I was talking about was beautiful and young; twenty years younger than my client to be exact, and greedy. She married my client for his money and he knew it. So to protect himself, he put five million dollars in escrow and had her sign a prenup that said she'd only get the money if she stayed with him and didn't cheat for five years. I guess he figured if he could have her to himself for five years, it was worth it, considering how hot she was and how rich he was. But the prenup also said if she did cheat during that time and he found out, she'd get nothing. So, understanding what she'd lose if she screwed around, she towed the line for the first three years and only had eyes for him. But in year four, because of their age difference, he started looking like shit. He got fat and lost his hair, and that's when he suspected she started having an affair. He was right, and after a couple days of surveillance I found her lover's house of infidelity and started my stake out. As I started my hundredth game of Angry Bird... "shit," a car came up the street and pulled into the driveway. A moment later my client's wife, wearing sunglasses and dressed in a long trench coat with a scarf covering her head, walked up to the door and knocked.

As she waited, I picked up my camera and started taking pictures; I provide my clients with photos to prove the cheating is real if the case goes to court. And even though she tried to disguise her appearance, I could tell it was her. She was tall and thin and moved her hips in a way that only happened in pornos, so I've heard, and the kind of girl you take home to meet dad, if he was still alive. A moment later a man opened the door and pulled her inside.

"Here we go," I said as I took the camera and snuck over to the house.

I took a position outside the master bedroom window where I knew I'd get the best shots, and watched as the woman stripped down to her bra and panties and the man stripped down to his boxers. I could see why she cheated. The guy was young, good-looking, and had a body that looked like he worked out twenty-four hours a day. He looked a lot like me; at least his eyelids did. As they started making out, I started taking pictures, and accidentally hit the window with the lens of my camera.

"Fuck," I said, hoping they hadn't heard the noise.

But they did, and looked toward the window.

"Oh shit!" I said as I started back to my car, tripped over a bush and fell on my back.

Before I could get up, the man, still in his boxers, ran out of the house followed by the woman wearing her trench coat again.

"Hey, motherfucker, who are you?" he said as he jumped on top of me.

"He's the private investigator my husband hired to catch me cheating and stop me from getting my money."

"Is that right, asshole?" he said as he punched me in the face.

"Yeah. And all the proof I need is in this camera. You want to see the pictures?" I asked, as I hit him in the head with the camera, knocked him out and headed back to my car.

"That was one expensive fuck, sweetheart," I said as I held up the camera, "it just cost you five million bucks."

I didn't mention it before, but I grew up and live in Los Angeles. And while the English translation is "City of Angels," trust me there are plenty of devils living here; which makes it an infidelity rich environment, and a perfect place to be a private investigator. While the city is large and spread out, the downtown is small with only a few office buildings. My office is on the fifth floor of one of the older, cheaper buildings, because that's all I can afford. See, I'm in a "feast or famine" business, which means when I have a paying client, I can "feast" and eat something besides TV dinners. When I don't, I'm "famished" and back to TV dinners again. I got to my office at nine the next morning. I usually get in at eight, but I had a few drinks to celebrate proving my client's wife was cheating, and I was a little hung over. Frequent celebration for no reason is something Italian/Mexicans do a lot, also in our DNA. As I walked off the elevator, wearing sunglasses to cover the black eye I got the night before, a man walked out of a hallway men's room.

"Hey Razor, you peeping Tom, you spend the night getting your jollies watching people screw?"

"Yeah. And your wife wants you to bring home some milk. And not the two-percent shit your girlfriend drinks either."

"Fuck you," he said as he flipped me the bird and walked into his office.

"You'd like that wouldn't you?" I replied, and continued down the hall to my office.

By the way, I want to go on record and say that guy is full of shit. I'm not a peeping Tom. I'm a licensed, professional, private investigator with a license to carry a concealed weapon, who just happens to do a lot of peeping. And besides, it's Sam, not Tom, peeping Sam.

Not only is my building old, but my office is small, just two rooms. The front room is where Betty, my sixty-five-year old office manager sits and deals with clients, and my office is in the back. As I walked in, Betty saw the sunglasses.

"Got clocked again, huh, Sam?"

"Yeah," I said, taking off the glasses.

"That's even better than the last one."

"Remind me to get another camera lens," I said as I handed her the camera. "And get the pictures developed, so I can get them to Peter. Any messages?"

"Two: your brother and your ex-wife. He wants you to call him and she wants to know where this month's alimony check is."

"Did you tell her it's in the mail?"

"No, before I could say anything, she told me not to give her the 'in the mail routine' again. She wants the cash and so do I."

"I know, I owe you a week's pay, and as soon as Peter gives me the money for those pictures, I'll pay you and my ex-wife. Unless, you'd rather I mail you a check."

"Not funny," she said.

Betty's been with the agency since it started. She was the wife of my dad's best friend and needed a job, and my dad needed a secretary. When my dad died she was going to retire, but decided to stay on. Thank God! She's great with clients and doesn't cost me much, when I'm able to pay her, so I figure she's supplementing her income with kick-backs from the camera lens company.

"I don't suppose I've got any appointments?"

"In fact, you do. A woman named Mary Whitfield. She called just before you walked in and is on her way up. She didn't say what it was about, but she sounded upset."

"Did she call in response to my phone book ad?"

"You mean the one that reads, 'When you need a great Dick at an affordable price, call Sam Razor?'

"That sounds cleverer every time I hear it," I said, smiling.

"No, she didn't mention that terrible ad, she was recommended by a former client, but didn't say who."

"No shit? A referral, that's great."

While I'd had quite a few clients through the years, I couldn't think of which one of them would tell someone else to use me. Don't get me wrong, I'm good, but not too recommendable.

"Get Peter on the phone for me, please," I said as I walked into my office and shut the door.

As I sat down at my desk and turned on my computer, Betty's voice came over the intercom.

"Sam, Mr. Bolman is on the phone."

"Hello, Peter ... yeah, I got the proof she violated your agreement ... yeah, she's screwed alright, literally. So, I'll come to your office this afternoon with the pictures, and pick up my check ... great, see you then," I said, and hung up the phone.

At that moment, Betty came over the intercom again.

"Sam, Miss Mary Whitfield, is here to see you."

"Bring her back."

A few seconds later, Betty came in escorting a gorgeous, thirty-year-old woman.

"Sam, this is Mary Whitfield."

While I had no idea who recommended me to this beauty, I was glad they did. She was a stunner. She was a tall, thin, blonde haired, blue-eyed beauty with a great body, and dressed in a suit that looked more expensive than my car.

"It's nice meeting you, Miss Whitfield," I said as I shook her hand.

"Please, call me Mary."

"Please, sit down, Mary," I said as I moved some folders off a chair in front of my desk. "Betty, can you bring us some coffee, please?"

"Not for me, Betty, but thank you."

"I'll have mine later, too, Betty, thanks." Betty left the office.

"So, Mary, what can I do for you?"

"Before we start, are you okay?"

At first, I didn't know what she was talking about. Then I realized she was referring to my black eye.

"Oh, this," I said, pointing at my eye. "I'm fine, just had a run in with an angry racket ball. I play four or five times a week to stay in shape," I said as I stuck out my chest to look more athletic.

Considering how fit she looked, I didn't want her to think

I was a slacker when it came to exercise; even though I was. Don't get me wrong, I do occasionally work out, I just couldn't remember the last occasion.

"My younger sister, Margret, is missing and I want to hire you to find out what happened to her."

"Missing? What do you mean?"

"We share a house in Las Vegas and she hasn't come home or called in a couple of days, and she's never done that before. We have an understanding that we let each other know if we're staying out all night and not coming home; being single, we watch out for each other. So, because she hasn't called, I think she's in trouble," she said, and started to cry. "I'm sorry. My sister and I are very close."

It usually bothered me to see a woman cry, but she was so beautiful I could have watched her cry through two verses of the National Anthem and asked for an encore.

"I understand, I'm close to my brother, too," I said, half-telling the truth. "What kind of trouble do you think she's in?" I asked, as I handed her a Kleenex.

"Thank you. She likes to party and hangs out in the casinos with some shady characters, so it could be anything."

"Maybe she just partied a little too hard and is sleeping it off somewhere before she comes home. Does she have a boyfriend?"

"She did, they just broke up. He's one reason I'm afraid she might have been," she paused and took a breath, "kidnapped."

When I heard the word "kidnapped" my ears perked up. Someone only gets kidnapped when there's a lot of money involved.

"Why do you suspect kidnapping?"

"My sister and I inherited a lot of money when our mother died in a car accident a couple of years ago, and I'm afraid someone is trying to get their hands on it."

"And you think it's her ex-boyfriend?"

"Maybe. I know he needs money and my sister refused to help him, so he might be trying to force me to give him the money to get her back."

"Have you gone to the police with your suspicions?"

"No. Considering the crowd my sister hangs around with, I don't want to get the police involved until I'm sure what's going on. That's why I came to you."

"You couldn't find an investigator a little closer to home?"

"I could, but you came so highly recommended by a friend of a friend, that I decided to talk to you first."

Highly recommended, now I knew it was the camera lens company.

"If your sister's been kidnapped, you should have gotten a ransom demand."

"What do you mean?"

"Normally, in a kidnapping there's a note or a call from the kidnapper confirming they have your sister, and how much money they want to give her back."

"Are you saying if I haven't gotten a ransom demand, something more terrible could have happened to her? Like mur ..." She stopped and started to tear up again.

"I didn't mean to upset you, I'm sure she's fine. We'll find her."

"We'll? Does that mean you'll take the investigation?"

"If you're okay with my fees," I said, hoping there wouldn't be a problem.

"What is your fee?"

"I charge six hundred dollars a day, plus expenses."

I normally only charged four hundred a day, but considering this might be a kidnapping involving a lot of money, I jacked up my fee a little. After she heard the fee, she reached into her purse, pulled out a wad of cash and put it on my desk.

"Let's make it a thousand a day? And I'll give you a week in advance. Is that okay?"

A beautiful woman wanted to give me a fist full of money, and she wanted to know if it was okay?

"And if you find my sister and bring her home safe, I'll give you a fifty thousand dollar bonus."

When she said fifty thousand dollars, I almost fell off my chair.

"Did you say fifty thousand dollars?" I asked, for clarification.

"Yes. I told you my sister's important to me."

"Okay. But before you hire me officially, you need to know that until now I've only handled divorce cases, you know, catching people cheating. So if it turns out to be a kidnapping, and the kidnapper isn't having an affair, I could be out of my depth."

"I have faith in you, Sam," she said as she reached over and squeezed my hand.

"I do too," I said, returning the squeeze.

"Great. The money I set on your desk is seven thousand dollars for the first week. I had a feeling we'd come to an agreement."

She wasn't just beautiful, she was smart, the perfect combination of beauty and brains. The kind you want to take home to your Mexican mother. DNA, remember?

"Then we've got a deal," I said as we shook hands and I put the money in my desk drawer, "when should I start?"

"Tomorrow. I'll book you on a flight to Vegas first thing in the morning," she said as she stood up to leave the office.

"One more thing, Mary," I said as I walked her to the door. "Can you remember which of my past clients recommended me? I'd like to thank them."

"I don't remember. Like I said, it was a friend of a friend

that you helped in a divorce case a couple of years ago. He said something about an ad in the phone book. So, I'll see you tomorrow," she said as she walked out of the office.

"I knew that ad was a winner," I said as I picked up the phone to call my brother.

I was sure Pepe was calling to find out when I was going to pay him back the money I borrowed a couple of months ago. The truth was that until I had a paying client, I couldn't pay him. But now that I had two paying clients, I wanted to pay him back, so I could borrow it again.

"Hey brother, how are you?" I asked, trying to make small talk when I got him on the phone. "I know, you've been more than patient and that's why I called, to tell you I've got your money … no shit. I'll be working with a new client for the next few days, so I'll come by your office next Monday and take you to lunch … yes, the money I owe you will be joining us. Goodbye."

Me and my brother spent our entire childhood getting each other in trouble. He was an easy target and was always doing something that I could use against him, like having girls in the house when my parents weren't home. No girls in the house was our dad's sacred rule, and one that Pepe was always breaking. And when he did, I'd blackmail him and threaten to tell my dad unless he did things for me. You know, like taking my turn doing the dishes or taking out the trash. Obviously, that pissed him off, and he'd try to get even, but it never worked. Since I was the baby of the family, my parents let me get away with murder. And when it came to my word against Pepe's, considering Dad didn't trust Pepe as far as he could throw him when it came to girls, he always took my word.

"You can't prove I had a girl in the house, you little squealer," he'd say. "And you know how Dad hates snitches without proof. So, you little prick, if you get me in trouble again without proof, I'll kick your ass," he said, clinching his fist.

Pepe was right. I was half his size, and he could easily kick the shit out of me, and did all the time. He was also right about Dad not wanting us to tattle on each other, unless it was something bad that we could prove, like girls in the house when he wasn't home. So that's when I started taking pictures. I told my dad I wanted to get into photography and needed a camera. Truth was, I didn't care about photography, I wanted the camera so I could get the visual proof I needed to prove to my dad Pepe had girls in the house. So, for my thirteenth birthday, my dad bought me a cheap Kodak, and I started my picture taking reign of terror. The next time our parents went out of town, and I knew Pepe was bringing a girl to the house, I hid under his bed and waited. As soon as his underwear was down around his ankles, and the girl's blouse was off, I rolled out from under the bed, took the picture and ran. I must admit, when I saw tits for the first time, I was so was mesmerized, I almost forget to take the picture.

"You come back here, you little prick, I'm going to kill you," Pepe screamed, as he tried to chase me and tripped over his underwear.

Then I hid the picture where I knew he wouldn't look, behind the toothpaste in the medicine cabinet, and threatened to show it to Dad if he didn't do what I wanted. And since I had the proof, and Pepe knew it, I didn't do dishes for the next month. That is, until my parents forced him to brush his teeth, and he found the picture and destroyed the evidence. Then he not only beat the shit out of me, he locked me in my pitch-black bedroom closet overnight. Pepe knew I had a bad case of claustrophobia and was terrified of small, tight, dark places, so being locked in the dark closet scared the shit out of me. But what scared me worse was that he threatened to do it every time I pissed him off from then on. So, as you can imagine, I spent most of my childhood in the closet and still break out in a rash when I get close to coat hangers.

CHAPTER TWO

THE LAND OF BAD BETS

The next day I landed in Vegas two hours late, which by current airline time standards is early, and I headed to baggage claim where Mary said her driver would pick me up. While I really like Vegas, I don't go very often because when I do I always end up losing my shirt. In fact, I had a case in Vegas a few years back involving a casino executive who was cheating on his wife, and I had to go undercover and pose as a bellhop. It took me a couple of weeks of carrying luggage before I got pictures of the executive having sex with a sexy showgirl in his office. And during that time, I played Blackjack every night and not only lost my shirt, but two pairs of pants, and four gold fillings; so you can see why I don't go to Vegas.

After I picked up my bags, I walked outside and put on my SPF1000, to keep from getting fried by the 120 degree heat, another reason I don't go to Vegas. I saw a driver holding a sign with my name on it.

"I'm Sam Razor."

"Nice meeting you, Sam. My name's Alex and I'm the sisters' driver. The car's right over here," he said as he took my bags and escorted me to a nearby limo.

I got into the limo and we headed out of the airport. The last time I was in a limo was on my wedding day and the memories of that weekend came rushing back. When my wife and I were first married we were madly in love, and thought we'd be in love forever. In fact, that's why they make you say, "till death do you part" during the ceremony, so you'll feel obligated to make it work, at least until after the honeymoon. Like I said, we met in high school and got married after just a couple of months of dating and I felt lucky to have her. Until I found out nine other guys were also lucky to have her, my friend included.

As we drove away from the airport, I could see Vegas had changed since the last time I was here. All the land that was just barren mounds of dirt last time, was now covered with houses, trees and grass; nothing like California you understand, but a definite improvement. We drove for a while and eventually entered a guard gated housing development several miles from the strip. This wasn't your typical, middle-American housing track. These were estates with their own gates and private driveways surrounded by acres of beautifully landscaped property.

"Man," I said to Alex, "these houses are spectacular."

"Yep. This is the most expensive development in Vegas. Only wealthy entertainers and prominent rich people can afford to live here."

As soon as I heard that, I knew Mary and her sister had the kind of money a kidnapper would go after, especially if he was a broke, jilted ex-lover. I also knew I should have jacked up my fee even more.

We drove past several estates and parked in front of a mansion that was bigger than my entire block in L.A. It was two stories and designed to look like a European castle, minus the moat and drawbridge. While the house didn't look like Mary's style, I figured her and her sister inherited it when their mother died. That arrangement was okay with me, because I was taught to never look a gift mansion in the mouth, no matter how ugly it was.

As Alex brought my luggage to the door, a sophisticated older man dressed in an expensive suit and tie stepped out.

"Mr. Razor?"

"That's right."

"It's a pleasure meeting you," he said, shaking my hand. "My name is Robert and I'm the Whitfield's personal valet."

Wow, Mary and her sister not only had a driver, they had their own butler. I always wanted a butler. A guy that would do everything for me including spending time with "Shut the Fuck Up" to expand his vocabulary.

"Mary's waiting for you in the backyard near the pool."

The inside of the mansion was decorated in the same ugly-ass European style as the outside with several overstuffed leather couches, a million old-world paintings, and a winding staircase. While it was obvious Mary's parents had a lot of money, they should have spent more of it on better taste. I followed Robert through the house and ended up in the backyard. Backyard? What am I talking about? It wasn't a yard, it was a field, complete with an Olympic size pool, several tennis courts, and a guesthouse almost as big as the mansion itself. When Mary saw me, she ran over.

"Sam, my sister was kidnapped. I got this ransom note

this morning," she said as she handed me a piece of paper. "It says the kidnapper will call me later today with the amount he wants to give her back. And if I don't cooperate or get the police involved, I'll never see her alive again," she said, tearfully.

"It came this morning?" I asked, studying the note.

"Yes, and this was with it," she said as she handed me a ring. "That's a ring I gave my sister for her twenty-first birthday. She never took it off."

The ring was a big-ass Ruby, and had an inscription on the inside of the band that read, "All my love, Mary."

"Any significance to the ring?"

"My sister's birthstone is the Ruby, and I had the ring made especially for her."

I couldn't believe my ears. Her sister turns twenty-one and gets an expensive piece of jewelry. When I turned twenty-one, I was living with my parents and just getting started in the business, so all I got was a cheap card and the "apartments for rent" section of the newspaper.

"What do we do now?"

"Well, now that we know for sure the kidnapper has your sister, we need to wait and find out what he wants. Did you think of anyone else, besides her ex-boyfriend, who would have a reason to kidnap her?"

"The only other person is Charles Jenkins. He's the owner of the Crystal Palace Casino and my mother's last husband. When he built the casino, he overspent big time and is having trouble paying his bills. He and my mother dated for a year after my dad's death, and he talked her into marrying him. She was so lonely without my dad, she agreed. But as soon as the wedding was over she found out about his money problems when he asked her to help finance the casino debt. She turned him down. And after she died and left everything to my sister and me, he stopped talking to us. So, he's desperate for money and he knows we have it."

"Is it just you and Margret? No other siblings?"

"We have an older brother, Michael, but my parents kicked him out of the house and disowned him several years ago."

"Why?"

"He was a drug addict and stole several priceless keepsakes from my parents to support his habit, so they threw him out."

"When was the last time you heard from him?"

"A couple of years ago. He got arrested and reached out to my mother for bail, but she didn't give it to him."

"Do you have a picture of him and your sister, so I'll know what they look like?"

"There aren't any pictures of my brother. My dad destroyed them all."

"He was that upset?"

"Yes. He was so angry with my brother, he didn't allow anything in the house that had anything to do with him."

I guess the father was angry; I'd heard of being disowned, but dis-pictured?

"The rest of our family photos are in my dad's study. I'll show you," she said as she led me into a study in the lower level of the house.

The study was huge. It housed at least a thousand books and tons of family and other photos of famous people ranging from politicians to movie stars.

"Wow, pretty impressive."

"My dad was a prominent attorney and represented some of the most famous people in the world. He loved this study and spent hours in here reading and thinking. I come in here every day and sit at his desk to remember him and my mom. It's still hard."

"I understand. My dad had a study, too"—*the downstairs bathroom*. I think about him every time I go in there," I said, as I remembered my dad sitting on the can. "Anyway, you were going to show me a picture of your sister."

"They're over here," she said as she walked to a shelf of family photos and picked up a picture of Mary and two other blonde women at a celebration.

"That's me, my sister Margret, and our mother, taken just a few weeks before my dad died, at my parents' fiftieth anniversary party."

"You're all beautiful."

"We take after our mother. She was beautiful, inside and out."

Even though Margret was beautiful and very sexy, as I looked closer I saw something slightly out of whack about her face, it was her nose. It was crooked and looked like she had botched plastic surgery.

"Did your sister have surgery on her nose?"

"Yes, she was driving my mother's car when the accident happened, and was thrown through the windshield. The plastic surgeons could repair her face, but that was the best they could do with her nose."

"Your sister was driving the car that killed your mother?"

"Yes. And even though they determined the accident was caused by a blown tire, she still blames herself."

"Please don't take this the wrong way, but did your mother and sister get along?"

"Why? Are you suggesting my sister had something to do with my mother's death?"

"No, I just want to know as much as I can about your

family's relationships with one another."

"My sister adored our mother and tried to commit suicide twice after she died."

"I'm sorry. Well, at least now I know what she looks like."

"So, what's your first step, Sam?"

"Well, while you wait to hear from the kidnapper about the ransom, I think I'll check into my hotel and then talk to Jenkins."

"I hope you don't mind, Sam, but I didn't book you a hotel. I thought it would be more convenient to stay here in the guesthouse. That way Alex can take you wherever you want to go and we can stay in touch. I hope that's alright?"

I had a hard and fast rule to not get close to my clients during an investigation, that way I wouldn't be interrupted constantly. But considering how upset Mary was, and how spectacular the house was, I decided to break the rule.

"That's great."

"Then I'll have Robert put your luggage in the guesthouse while you're gone. Sam, should we consider getting the police involved? I want to make sure I'm doing everything I can to get her home safe."

Don't get me wrong, I think the police do a great job, just ask Pepe. But before I got them involved, I wanted to investigate on my own first, especially considering there was fifty-grand at stake.

"Not yet. Let me do some investigation first and see what I can find out. We don't want to risk your sister's life. You okay with that?"

"Of course. You're right," she said as she took my hand. "Thank you again for your help, Sam. And I'm sorry if I got upset."

"And I'm sorry if it sounded like I was accusing your sister of anything."

"It's okay. I know you're just doing your job."

"And don't worry, we'll get your sister home safe."

"I hope so."

"Well, I want to get started," I said as I walked out of the study. "So, I'll see you later."

With that, me and Alex headed to the Crystal Palace to talk to Jenkins. As soon as Mary knew we were gone, she picked up her cell phone.

"He's on his way."

CHAPTER THREE

A REAL FUCKER

As I thought more about Mary's reaction to my question about the relationship between her sister and mother, something bothered me. Since the sisters didn't inherit the money until the mother was dead, was it possible the accident wasn't an accident? And since Mary stood to inherit all the money if her sister was out of the picture, did she have something to do with it and intended for her sister to be killed, too? And while that possibility didn't make sense, considering how close Mary was to her mother and sister, Chapter One of the P.I. Manual says to suspect everybody no matter how beautiful and sexy she is.

We hadn't driven very far from the mansion, when Alex rolled down the driver's partition.

"Sam, I think someone's following us," he said. "They've been behind us since we left the mansion."

I turned around and saw a black Mercedes with dark

tinted windows.

"Do you recognize the car?"

"No. In Vegas everyone owns a black Mercedes, I think it's a state law," he said, smiling.

"Slow down and see if they pass us," I said as I moved close to the window to get a better look.

We slowed down and the Mercedes did pass us. But because of the dark tint on the windows, all I could see was the silhouette of two people in the front seat, but couldn't make out if they were men or women.

"Should I follow them, Sam?"

"No, let's head to the Crystal Palace. I got a feeling we'll see them again."

We got to the Crystal Palace and I had Alex wait in the car while I went in to meet with Jenkins. The inside of the casino certainly lived up to its name, there was crystal everywhere you looked. Crystal pillars, crystal gambling tables, and crystal chips. But the thing that stood out the most was the huge rotating crystal chandelier in the center of the lobby. Mary was right, the place obviously cost Jenkins a fortune; it takes a shit load of money to get that much ugly-ass crystal in one place. The casino was crowded, and as I walked toward the front desk all I could hear were the sounds of slot machines gobbling up people's life savings. Remember, I said I wasn't a big gambler, but I didn't say I didn't gamble at all. So, as I passed a slot machine, I stuck in a dollar and hit a small payoff. As I collected my winnings, I heard a seductive woman's voice.

"Looks like it's your lucky day, handsome."

I looked up and saw a gorgeous, young blonde who was obviously all female and even more hooker.

"Want to make it even luckier?" she said as she winked at me.

"Thanks for the offer," I said as I put my winnings in my pocket, "but I've got an appointment."

"Then maybe I'll see you later," she said as she walked up to another guy sitting at a nearby bar.

As I walked up to a desk clerk, I decided in the future not to get married again and just use hookers, they'd cost me less.

"Welcome to the Crystal Palace, sir," the desk clerk said. "Can I help you?"

"I'm looking for the management offices."

"First elevator on your right, fifty-fifth floor."

"Fifty-fifth floor, huh?" I said as my claustrophobia kicked in and I remembered my closet.

As I got in the elevator, I saw the elevator walls were glass and showed the inside of the casino as it went up. I didn't mention it before, but besides being claustrophobic, I'm also afraid of heights. My mother says I take after her father, he would get sick to his stomach sitting on a tall barstool. I'm not that bad, tall barstools don't bother me, but short ladders are another story.

"Holy shit!" I said as I started to sweat and took several deep breaths.

I don't know who designed elevators with glass walls, but if I didn't know better, I'd swear it was my asshole brother. The ride to the top took about a minute, thank God, and I walked out into a mirror-covered corridor that looked like a circus sideshow. And while the elevator didn't make me sick, the three thousand images of myself almost did. So I kept my eyes on the floor and walked down the corridor and through a door labeled Crystal Palace Executive Offices. I was relieved to see the inside office walls weren't covered with mirrors, and I started to relax. But the relief didn't last long when I realized the reason there weren't any mirrors was because all the walls were twenty-foot high, floor to ceiling windows overlooking the entire Vegas strip. It felt like I was standing outside on the ledge of the building and I almost passed out. As I backed away from the windows, and looked back at the floor, I knocked over a lobby chair.

"Can I help you, sir?"

I raised my eyes and came face-to-face with a seven foot, four hundred pound security guard; he was so big, he had his own zip code.

"I'm here to see Mr. Jenkins," I said, looking down again.

"Follow-me," he said as he escorted me to a reception desk.

"This guy's here to see the boss," the security guard said to a female receptionist.

"Do you have an appointment, sir?"

"No, but I'm a friend of his stepdaughter, Mary Whitfield."

"And your name?"

"Sam Razor."

"Just give a minute and I'll see if he's available to see you, Mr. Razor," she said as she picked up a phone and dialed.

As she turned away and whispered into the phone, I accidentally looked out one of the windows and started to get dizzy again. As I took a deep breath and steadied myself against the desk, the receptionist turned back to me.

"Please follow me, Mr. Razor," she said as she led me to an interior office at the end of another long, mirrored hallway, and knocked on the office door.

"Come in," came a man's voice from inside the office.

I opened the door and walked into an office surrounded by the same windows, and decorated with pictures of movie stars and the same ugly-ass crystal statues I saw in the lobby. Charles

Jenkins, a sophisticated looking older man walked over to me. From the looks of this guy, I could tell he thought he was Mr. Las Vegas. He was more manicured than the greens on a PGA golf course and was wearing an expensive, designer black silk suit. I knew it was designer, because living in L.A, you see a lot of designer clothes. Everywhere you look you see people wearing Armani and Gucci. In fact, I had a couple Armani suits myself; Pedro Armani no relation to Giorgio.

"Mr. Razor, it's nice to meet you," Jenkins said, as he shook my hand. "Please, sit down," he said as he sat back at his desk.

As I walked over and sat in a chair in front of his desk, I looked at the floor to keep from looking out the windows.

"So, you're a friend of Mary's?"

"Well actually, I'm a private investigator, hired by Mary to find out who kidnapped her sister," I said, wanting to see his reaction.

"Margret's been kidnapped?" he said with seemingly genuine shock.

"You mean you didn't know?"

"How would I? I haven't spoken to the girls in over a month. When did it happen?"

"A couple of days ago."

"Do you have any idea who's responsible?"

"That's what I'm trying to find out. You say you haven't talked to Mary and her sister in a while?"

"That's right. After their mother died we went our separate ways."

"Did your 'going your separate ways' have anything to do with their mother leaving all her money to Mary and her sister and nothing to you?"

"Boy, you don't waste any time, do you?"

"It's a kidnapping, so I don't have time to waste."

"So, Mary told you about my financial problems?"

"Yeah."

"Well, I won't it deny it, I did spend a lot more money than I wanted on the casino. Vegas is a tough place to do business and unless you stand out and attract attention the competition will eat you up. But to be honest, it wasn't the cost. I underestimated how long it would take for the casino to make money, and some of my investors want their money back. I also won't deny that I hoped Mary's mother would invest and bail me out. But contrary to popular opinion, that wasn't why I married her. Look Sam, can I call you Sam?"

"Sure, Charles."

"I might have some financial challenges, but I'm not desperate or stupid enough to consider kidnapping. Besides, I have an alibi. I was in Europe and just got back this morning."

"I suppose somebody can corroborate that?"

"My secretary went with me, she'll tell you."

Even though I didn't want to believe him, he sounded sincere. I mean, he was honest about his financial problems and his relationship with Mary's mother, and if he was trying to hide something, why would he be so forthcoming with his information? But it didn't make any difference, because I was sure his "sex-retary" would support his story.

"I don't suppose you'd have any idea who would want to kidnap Margret?" I asked, probing.

"Could be a few people. I'm sure Mary told you that Margret's wild and runs around with some real slimeballs; drug dealers, loan sharks and underworld types."

"How do you know that?"

"She comes into the casino with a lot of different guys."

"Mary told me that Margret and her boyfriend recently

broke up. Is he one of the guys?"

"Yeah. Tommy 'the Broker' Dietrich, a small-time mobster. Rumor has it him and Margret were hot and heavy, but broke up after he slapped her around for flirting with other guys."

"Is he also financially challenged?"

"Yeah. Rumor also has it he owes a lot of money to the mob and they're threatening to kill him if he doesn't pay it back."

"Sure are a lot of rumors about the guy," I said, suspiciously. "Why do they call him the Broker?"

"Because he has a reputation of breaking people's arms."

"I hope that isn't instead of shaking hands," I said, smiling. "Is he in the casino a lot?"

"He plays craps here every night around midnight."

"Well, then don't be surprised if you see me in the casino later tonight."

"That's fine, Sam, but be careful, I don't want any trouble."

"Don't worry," I said as I got up and walked to the office door, "I'm fond of my arms just the way they are."

CHAPTER FOUR

KEEPING SCORE

On the ride back to Mary's, I kept replaying my meeting with Jenkins. Even though he seemingly had an airtight alibi and said kidnapping wasn't his style, debt has a way of bringing things back in style real fast. And now there was Tommy the Broker. And if the rumors were true about his financial problems, he had a few reasons for kidnapping Margret, and they all started with the words "mob-payback." And even though I hadn't met him yet, I already didn't like him. I hated guys who hit women; they were either cowards or ran around with smaller women than I did. When I got back to the mansion, I could hear the muffled sounds of Mary yelling from her father's study. I walked into the study and found her sitting at her father's desk talking on the telephone.

"I can't get that much money by then, I need more time," she said as she slammed down the receiver and started to cry.

"The kidnapper?"

"Yes, and he wants ten million dollars in unmarked bills in two days or my sister dies."

"Ten million dollars?" I said as I tried to wrap my mind around what that much money looked like, but couldn't get past a hundred. "Do you have access to that much money?"

"Yes, my parents' estate is valued at fifty million, but the money's in a trust that only allows me and my sister to take five hundred thousand dollars a year, unless there's an emergency and we both agree in writing. That way one of us can't get more of the money without the other one knowing."

I couldn't believe my ears, Mary and her sister were worth fifty million and only allowed to take five hundred thousand a year. What a shame. My parents' estate was worth a whopping fifty dollars, and set up so my brother and I could only take five dollars a year so neither one of us could spend the whole fifty bucks at one time.

"So your sister would have to agree in writing to get the ransom money?"

"Yes. Do you think the kidnapper will go along with that?"

"Sounds like he doesn't have much choice. Did he tell you where to deliver the money?" I asked.

"No, he said he'd contact me again tomorrow. And he warned me again not to get the police involved."

"Then we'll tell him about needing your sister's signature when we talk to him. I don't suppose you recognized the kidnapper's voice? Did it sound like Jenkins or the Broker?"

"I couldn't tell, it was disguised. This is a nightmare, Sam," she said as she started to cry.

"Listen," I said as I put my arm around her shoulder to comfort her, "everything's going to work out, I promise."

"Thank you, Sam, I really appreciate your being here. You must be starving. Let's have dinner and you can tell me about your meeting with Charles."

"Sounds good."

While we had dinner, I filled her in on my meeting with Jenkins. I could tell I was hob-knobbing with real wealth because the meal was served on real plates instead of T.V. dinner trays.

"He was an interesting character. He confirmed his financial problems and his relationship with your mother, which he said wasn't about money. And he also said he genuinely loved her and you and your sister."

"That's bullshit. That asshole never cared for us. I told you he was only with my mother for her money."

"She must have had some feelings for him."

"No, he was nothing more than a companion. He and my dad were partners on a few real estate deals and after my dad's death, my mother kept the business going and a year later her and Charles got married. But like I said, as soon as he knew he wasn't in my mother's will, he dumped us faster than you could say slimeball. Believe me, Sam, the guy can't be trusted."

"He also told me about the Broker's money problems. He said Tommy owes the mob money and they want it back, or he dies. So it turns out your suspicions about both the Broker and Jenkins were right, they both have money motives to kidnap your sister."

"But which one did it?"

"That's what I need to find out, and Tommy's next on my list to talk to. Jenkins said he plays Craps at The Crystal Palace every night, so I'm going back there tonight."

"You have to be careful, Sam, Tommy's dangerous."

"I heard," I said as I looked at my arms. "I'll meet you in

the morning for breakfast and tell you what I find out."

"That sounds good."

"And if the kidnapper contacts you again tonight, make sure to call me," I said as I got up from the table.

"I will. Goodnight and good luck."

"Goodnight," I said, as I left the house.

CHAPTER FIVE

AS CLEAR AS A MUD

Time was running out. If I wanted the fifty grand bonus, I needed to find Margret before something happened to her, since I knew Mary wouldn't agree to renegotiating a dead or alive deal. Alex drove me back to the Crystal Palace and waited outside again while I went in. The casino was still packed at twelve o'clock as I walked toward the craps tables. If I was in L.A., I would have been in bed for hours by this time, especially if my right hand had a headache. But in Vegas, sleeping was a waste of time, and like every other poor schmuck, I looked forward to winning that fortune I knew was just the next bet away. Before I got to the craps tables, I stopped at a bar to get a drink, and the gorgeous hooker from earlier in the day walked up and sat down next to me.

"Remember me?"

"I never forget a beautiful woman. Can I buy you a drink?"

"Sure," she replied, and signaled the bartender, "Frank,

bring me my usual, please."

"I take it you're here a lot?"

"I'm in all the casinos a lot, but I get more business from this one," she replied, as the bartender brought her a martini.

"Cheers," she said as we touched glasses.

"Cheers. Can I ask you a question?"

"Don't worry, I don't charge a lot," she said jokingly.

"But I do," I said, returning the joke. "You ever heard of Tommy Dietrich?"

The second she heard Tommy's name, she looked concerned.

"You mean, the Broker?"

"Yeah."

"All the girls on the street know Tommy."

"Is that right?"

"Yeah, he has a reputation for liking rough sex."

"Rough? Like in slapping the girls around?"

Her expression turned from concern to fear as she paused.

"I don't know," she said, in a way that told me she did know, but was afraid to say, "Why are you asking about Tommy?"

"I'm supposed to meet him and was told he hangs out in here."

"Yeah, he's at a craps table right now. So you've never met him?"

"No, why?"

"Well, he's not a nice man, so be careful."

"Thank you, I will."

"So, how did your meeting go today?" she asked, changing the subject.

"It was good. And how was your day?"

"Great, but spending time with you tonight would make it even better," she said as she moved closer to me and put her hand on my thigh. "You up for it?"

Up for it? Any further up, I would have been hanging out. But just as I was considering her proposition, Jenkins walked up.

"Sam, it's good to see you again. And I see you brought a friend," he said as he gave the hooker a dirty look.

"Ah, no, I'm here by myself," I said as I moved her hand off my thigh.

"That's right," the hooker said, "I was just asking him if he had a cigarette, but he doesn't smoke. Don't suppose you do?" she asked Jenkins

"No, and you know I don't like hookers hanging around my casino harassing my customers. Now get the fuck out of here," he said as he signaled a couple of plain-clothed security guards.

"See you around, handsome," she said as she finished her drink and was escorted out of the casino.

"You got to be careful, Sam. A lot of hookers in Vegas are undercover cops trying to bust guys for solicitation."

While I heard what he said, I decided there was no way the hooker was a cop. But if she was, then bring on the strip and deep cavity searches.

"Come on," Jenkins said, "I'll introduce you to the Broker."

We walked up to a craps table occupied by one casually dressed, good-looking man in his thirties with a stack of thousand dollar chips in front of him, and stood on either side of his chair.

"Tommy," said Jenkins, "it's good to see you again."

"Don't give me that shit," Tommy said, not looking up. "You mean it's good to see me losing money again."

"That too," said Jenkins, smiling. "Tommy, I want you to meet Sam Razor. He's a private investigator working for Mary."

"Is that right?" Tommy said, not looking at me, "That bitch can use a private dick," he said as he grabbed his crotch.

"And I've got just the one for her."

"Well it looks like you two gentlemen have a lot to talk about, so I'll leave you alone. And Sam, I'm sure we'll be talking," Jenkins said as he walked away from the table.

"Count on it," I said to him as I watched Tommy lose another bet.

"You play craps, Razor?"

"No, blackjack is more my game."

"Blackjack's for pussies," he said as he placed another bet. "But you're not here to discuss the finer points of casino games. Are you, Razor?"

"No, I'm here to find out if you know who kidnapped Mary's sister."

The question caught him off-guard and he finally looked at me.

"Margret's been kidnapped?" he said, in a way that, like Jenkins, sounded like fake surprise.

"That's right."

"When?"

"A couple of days ago. In fact, I think it was the same night I heard you beat her up."

Like the kidnapping statement, this statement caught him off-guard again, but this time he turned red and started to get angry.

"Is that what that bitch Mary told you? That I beat the shit out of her sister?" he said, as he clinched his fist and moved close to me.

"That's the story I got from a couple of people," I said, backing away and putting my hand on my gun.

"Well, they're all lying," he said as he regained his composure and unclenched his fist. "I ain't saying we don't fight, but I would never do anything to hurt her. I love her. Have you seen her, Razor?"

"Just her picture."

"Well she's even better looking than Mary and twice as sexy. Guys are always coming on to her and she loves to make me jealous. I admit, I've got a bad temper, but I've never lost it with her," he said, trying to sound sincere.

"Not even when she refused to help you with your financial problems?"

The fact that I knew about his money problems, and was insinuating that was the reason he kidnapped Margret made him angry again.

"I don't know what the fuck you're talking about. I don't have financial problems and even if I did, I would never think about kidnapping."

So now both Jenkins and the Broker claimed they wouldn't stoop to kidnapping to solve their financial problems, but my gut told me one of them was lying. And for the moment, considering how dangerous Tommy was, and that he was standing next to me, and probably had a gun, I chose to believe him.

"Come on, let me buy you a drink," he said, regaining his calm demeanor and smiling, "and I'll tell you anything else you want to know."

He picked up the remainder of his chips and led me to a table in a nearby bar.

"What's your poison?" he asked as a female server walked up.

"Scotch and water."

"Give me my usual, Doll."

As the server walked away, Tommy looked at me.

"So, how do you know Margret's been kidnapped?"

I figured he already knew, but I told him about the ransom note and the money the kidnapper asked for so I could watch his reaction.

"Ten million dollars? That's a lot of money," he said, in a way that verified he already knew.

"But Mary can't get the money unless her sister agrees in writing."

While the kidnapping and ransom information didn't get a reaction from him, the signature information did, and his demeanor changed from calm to concern.

"Well, I suppose that makes sense, considering how much money that is," he said, as the server brought our drinks.

"I also talked to your friend Jenkins today," I said, trying to see if him and Jenkins had a connection.

"That prick's no friend of mine. He's a crook," he said, trying to shift the focus to Jenkins, "and can't be trusted. I've done business with him a couple of times in the past and both times he tried to fuck me. The asshole would screw over his mother if she had something he wanted. I'm sure Mary told you about his money problems?"

"Yeah."

Since it didn't sound like Tommy and Jenkins were in on the kidnaping together, I shifted the focus back to Tommy.

"So let me ask you, when was the last time you saw Margret?"

"Three nights ago. We went to dinner and then came here to gamble. We both had a lot to drink and got into an argument, and she decided to go home. So I put her in a cab and I stayed and played craps."

"I suppose somebody can corroborate that?"

"Yeah, the pit boss on duty that night will tell you that she left by herself and I stayed."

I figured the pit boss must be on his payroll and, like Jenkins' secretary, would say anything Tommy wanted him to, so I decided there was no reason to verify his story.

"And you haven't seen or heard from her since that night?"

"No, but she does that sometimes after an argument. She says she needs time away to cool off. And to tell you the truth I don't mind, the absence may make my dick grow fonder, if you know what I mean." he said, smiling.

I knew exactly what he meant, as I thought about the hooker again.

"Is there anything I can do to help you find her?" he asked, as he finished his drink.

I wanted to say, "Sure, just give her back." But since there was ten million dollars at stake, I knew he wouldn't go along with that, so I played along.

"I appreciate the offer," I said as I finished my drink and stood up to leave, "but I think it's better if I handle this alone."

"I understand," he said as he took out a business card reading Tommy "The Broker" Dietrich, Financial Analyst, and handed it to me. "If I can be of help, Sam, don't hesitate to call. And by the way, do you know why they call me the Broker?" he asked, moving close to me.

"No," I said nervously, as I moved my arms behind my back and put my hand on my gun again.

"It's because I'm a licensed stockbroker," he said, smiling. "So, if you ever need any stock tips, just let me know," he said, reaching his hand out to shake.

"I will, thanks," I said as I shook his hand and started to walk away.

At that moment, Tommy's cell phone rang.

"Hello."

As Tommy listened to the person on the phone, he turned away from me and whispered so I couldn't hear his conversation. Since eavesdropping is another skill you learn as a P.I., I stopped walking and pretended to be looking for something in my pocket. But before I could hear anything, he put his hand over the phone receiver and looked back at me.

"Then, ah, I'll wait to hear from you," he said, obviously wanting me to leave.

"Absolutely," I replied as I smiled and walked out of the bar.

His behavior made me suspicious. I was sure he was talking about the kidnapping, and saying that Mary couldn't get the ransom money without her sister's signature, so I decided to tail him and find out. I walked to a blackjack table that had a clear view of Tommy and watched as he finished his call, walked out of the bar, and headed for the front door of the casino. Since I make my living following cheaters, I'm an expert at tailing people without them knowing. So I followed Tommy out of the casino, and while he waited for the valet to bring his car, I snuck over to the limo and got in.

"You can head home, Alex. I'm going to stay and gamble. Tell Mary I'll take a cab back to the house later."

"You sure, Sam?"

"Yeah, you've worked enough for one day. I'll see you tomorrow morning," I said, as I got out of the limo, walked over to a taxi line and got in one of the cabs.

I decided it was better following Tommy in a cab instead of the limo, especially if he was the one following me earlier and might recognize the car. Besides, I didn't want Alex to get hurt if things got rough. After all, I'm a licensed professional, trained to handle tough situations; don't forget how well my eye handled the boyfriend's fist. As I watched Tommy, the valet brought up a black Porsche and Tommy got in and drove off.

"Follow that Porsche," I said to my Pakistani cabdriver

slowly, hoping he understood English enough to know what I meant, and hoping Tommy would go the speed limit, so we could keep up with him.

Tommy went the speed limit all right, at the Indy Five Hundred. The asshole took off like a rocket and left us so far behind I had to look out the window to make sure we were moving. We followed him away from the strip to a residential section of town and watched as he parked in front of a run-down house. I figured the house was a hide-out and not where Tommy lived, because the only degenerates I knew that drove hundred thousand dollar cars and lived in shacks were drug dealers and not mobsters. No, my detective instincts told me this shack was home to a kidnapping, so I had the cabdriver park the cab down the street.

"Wait here and keep the engine running," I said slowly agian, as Tommy got out of his car and went into the house.

"No problem," replied the driver with a perfect English accent. "I'll keep the meter running, too," he said, smiling.

Figures, I said to myself, as I got out of the cab, pulled out my gun, and walked toward the house.

The house was dark and all the windows, except for one in the kitchen, were covered with cardboard. Since there was a light on in the kitchen, I could see Tommy and another man sitting at the kitchen table. As I walked around to the side of the house, I saw the cardboard was off one of the basement windows, so I got down on my hands and knees and looked inside. The basement was dark, but I could see the silhouette of a woman tied to a chair in the center of the room. I knew it was a woman, because of the two lumps sticking out from her chest, and if it was a woman, I assumed it was Margret. And since she was tied to the chair, I also assumed she was being held against her will, which is a sign of either a kidnapping or some kinky basement sex. I didn't see anyone else in the room, so I decided I could either confront Tommy and his partner head on and maybe get shot, or I could sneak into the basement through the window and sneak Margret out of the house before they knew what was happening. The window was just big enough for me to crawl through so I tried to pry it open, but it wouldn't budge. Turns out it was nailed shut so someone like me couldn't pry it open. So I decided to do what I'd seen done a thousand times in movies when someone wants to break a pane of glass without making noise. I covered the butt of my gun with the sleeve of my jacket and tapped the window with a sharp, quick blow and it worked like a charm. The glass broke, and just like in the movies, didn't make noise. But while the glass breaking wasn't noisy, the pieces of glass falling on the basement floor sounded like a fat man falling through a plate glass window, and immediately the light in the basement came on. I quickly moved away from the window and watched as Tommy came running down the basement stairs with his gun drawn. Now that the lights were on, I could see the woman was blonde and blindfolded, with her mouth and body duct-taped. Tommy checked her to make sure she was still secure and then walked over to the broken window.

"What the fuck?" he said as he picked up a piece of the glass and looked up at the broken window.

As I ducked out of sight, Tommy ran up the basement stairs. I figured he'd come out of the house through the front door, so I ran the several feet across the street and hid behind a parked car. Remember I said I worked out occasionally, well I guess I forgot to tell my lungs, because it took me a couple minutes to catch my breath, after all it was several feet. I watched as Tommy and his partner came out of the house, and ran over to the broken window.

They examined the window then split up and started looking around the rest of the house. As soon as they were both out of sight, I ran back to the broken window, crawled inside the basement, ran over to Margret and tried to remove the tape from her mouth. As I did, she started to flail around and mumble.

"Be quiet," I said, "they'll hear you, they're right outside. My name's Sam Razor and I'm a private investigator hired by your sister to find you and bring you home. So sit still so I can get the tape off and get you out of here before they come back."

She was covered in so much tape, I couldn't take it off with just my hands, so I looked around and found a small saw. As I started to cut the tape, she got agitated again and mumbled frantically. Realizing she was trying to warn me about something, I took out my gun and started to turn around, but before I could, I was hit in the head and knocked out.

CHAPTER SIX

THE RIGHT ANSWERS TO THE WRONG QUESTIONS

I didn't have a clue how long I was out, but I woke up to the shock of ice-cold water being thrown in my face. It felt like being pushed into an ice-cold swimming pool and almost having your heart stop and your balls shrivel up. Anyway, as soon as I was awake, I tried to move and realized I was sitting in a chair with my arms, legs, and mouth all duct-taped. As the fear of not being able to breathe kicked in and triggered my claustrophobia, I panicked and struggled to get free. As I did, I remembered Margret and looked over to see if she was alright, and did a double take. Instead of Margret, I saw Tommy slouched over in a chair next to me with a bullet hole in his head.

Having never been this close to a murder victim before, especially one with the back of his head blown off, I started to get sick to my stomach. I didn't realize that extreme fear causes your bladder to lose control and makes you piss your pants, but it does and I did. I thanked God that Pepe dealt with this kind of thing instead of me. In my line of work, cheaters only threatened to kill their spouses, and usually with a frying pan. Seeing the kidnapper was willing to commit murder, I figured it was better to stop struggling and try to find Margret, but she was nowhere in sight.

Suddenly, everything I suspected about Tommy wasn't adding up. If he was dead and Margret was gone, then Tommy was either double-crossed or was just a fall guy for the kidnapping and had served his purpose. But where was Margret? Since Tommy couldn't help me get free, given his corpse condition, and there wasn't anything in the P.I. Manual about removing duct-tape from yourself, I wasn't sure what the fuck to do next.

Knowing Tommy's partner was the one who threw water in my face, and that I was still alive, I figured he must want to talk to me before he killed me. And as I tried again to loosen the duck-tape from my hands, a black-haired, black-eyed man, in his thirties, wearing jeans and a t-shirt, came down the stairs wearing gloves and carrying a gun.

"I see you're awake," he said, as he walked over to me and ripped the duct-tape off my mouth.

Not having experienced the pain that comes from having an industrial adhesive ripped off your skin, and especially your face, I decided it felt like being hit in the balls with a Tiger Woods tee shot. As I fought back a scream, wanting to at least act like I was a real man, I licked my lips to make sure they were still attached.

"Who are you? And where's Margret?" I asked.

"What's the matter, Sam, can't figure it out? I know who

you are," he said, as he held up my investigator identification card from my wallet. "You're the private investigator Mary hired to get Margret back. And me, I'm Michael, the long-lost, disowned, drugged out brother, back in town to collect my rightful inheritance."

"And you had to kidnap your own sister and kill Tommy to do it?"

"What can I say? Tommy became a liability, and since I never got along with my sisters, I knew Mary wouldn't just give me the ten million by saying please, so I gave her some incentive."

"Is Margret still alive?"

"She's still alive and a long way from here. In fact, she was never here."

"What are you talking about? I saw her."

"Sam, for an investigator, your powers of observation aren't very good, are they? The woman you thought was Margret was really my girlfriend Diane," he said as he walked back to the bottom of the stairs and called out, "Diane, come down here and meet our new friend."

A moment later, the blonde I mistook for Margret walked down the stairs. Seeing her face without the blindfold and duck-tape, I could tell she wasn't Margret. Her nose was too perfect, but she was sexy.

"Sam, meet Diane, my accomplice."

"Don't call me an accomplice, Michael."

"Shut up, bitch. I'll call you anything I want."

"I never wanted to be involved with this. The whole thing was your idea."

"I said, shut the fuck up," he said as he slapped her hard across the face. "She's a little upset," he said to me, "but she'll be better when we get the ransom money."

The P.I. Manual chapter I did read several times, was the one on using fear tactics to get an unwilling person nervous enough to help you. I used it a lot when I tried to get cheaters to admit they were having an affair. I would tell them that if they didn't admit it, I'd turn them over to the police. I was lying, but the threat worked every now and then, especially if the cheater wasn't very smart; and in this case, my instincts told me Diane was the perfect unwilling person.

"You don't have to do this, Diane," I said.

"Shut the fuck up," Michael said.

"Kidnapping is a serious crime, Diane," I continued. "You can go to jail for the rest of your life if you're caught."

"What's he talking about, Michael? I don't want to go to jail for the rest of my life," she said, starting to cry.

"That's real fucking stupid," he said as he put another piece of duct tape over my mouth, "because now you've lost your speaking privileges."

"Is he right, Michael?"

"If we get caught, but that's not going to happen. And to make sure, I'll eliminate the only eyewitness right now," he said, as he walked over to me, pointed the gun at my head and cocked the trigger.

We've all heard stories about people seeing their life flash before their eyes right before they died, but up until that moment I never believed it.

I used to think, what was the point? What if your life was boring or you were alone or sick? Why would you want to relive all that sadness? But I was wrong. At the time of death, your mind does flash on familiar images of the people you love and the good times you've had, so death is easier to accept. The only thing that would have been better, was if I could have picked the images I wanted to see. I would have picked Mary, in a see-through negligée, but instead I saw my mother's body in a negligée, with Mary's head; it made me wish for a speedy death. As I closed my eyes and prepared for the end, Michael started to laugh.

"Open your eyes, Sam, I'm not going to kill you," he said, smiling. "I've got plans for you. I want you to be my delivery boy and deliver the ransom money to me."

I was so relieved that he wasn't going to kill me, I opened my eyes just as he ripped the duck tape off my mouth again. But this time I didn't mind the pain, because at least I was still alive to feel it.

"You won't get away with this," I said, feeling a little cocky now that I knew he wasn't going to kill me.

"Sure I will, and you're going to make sure I do, unless you want Margret to end up like Tommy."

"It's just a matter of time before the police find Tommy's body and start investigating."

"I'm not worried about that," he said as he took off the rest of the duck-tape. "He's a known mobster and they're always getting murdered and the police don't give a shit. But if you're thinking about going to the police, you better think again. Because besides a dead Margret, they'll find the murder weapon," he said, smiling holding up the gun, "which is registered to you and has your fingerprints on it,"

He had me. A dead Margret and my gun added up to a fucked Sam and he knew it. After he finished removing the rest of the tape, he pointed the gun at my head again.

"Now, you go and remind Mary that I want the unmarked ten million by tomorrow, to be delivered by you to a place I'll tell you about later."

"But I told Tommy Mary can't get the money unless Margret signs a release."

"I know, he told me. That's too bad, because if she can't figure a way to get it without her sister's signature, she'll get Margret back in ten million pieces. Am I making myself clear?" he asked, pointing his gun at Tommy's body.

"Crystal."

"Good. Now give us a ten minute head start and then you can leave. And Sam, don't be stupid and try to follow us. You don't have time to waste," he said as he and Diane left the house.

CHAPTER SEVEN

I WAS THE BAG MAN, BUT MY SHOES DIDN'T MATCH MY BAG

Fortunately, the cab driver waited, but unfortunately he did keep his meter running, and by the time we got to back to Mary's, the fare was almost as much as the ransom. When I walked into the house, Mary met me at the door and saw my condition.

"Sam, what happened to you? Are you all right?"

"I'm okay, but the Broker's been murdered."

"What? By whom?"

"Your brother, Michael."

"My brother? That's not possible, he's in jail."

"Apparently not. I followed Tommy to a house outside of town where I thought he was keeping your sister, but as it turned out she wasn't there. It was all part of a plan to get me to the house so your brother could force me to be the delivery boy for the ransom. He's the real mastermind behind the kidnapping and just used Tommy to help him get your sister."

"But why?"

"To force you to give him his share of the inheritance."

"So you're telling me that my drug addict brother somehow got out of jail and kidnapped my sister?"

"Looks that way."

"Is Margert still alive?"

"He said she is, but if he doesn't get the ten million in unmarked bills by tomorrow she won't be."

"Did you tell him that I can't get the money unless Margret signs a release?"

"He knows, but he doesn't care. He said for you to figure it out."

As Mary processed what she just heard, she had to sit down.

"Sam, I think it's time to get the police involved, they've got more resources, and will have a better chance of finding Margret."

"We can't do that. He threatened again to kill Margret if we did, and from what I saw, he'll do it. And there's something else."

"What?"

"He's got my gun, and if we don't do as he says, he'll use it to kill your sister and frame me for her murder."

"I can't believe this is happening," she said, starting to cry.

"Mary, can I ask you a question?"

"Sure, Sam, anything."

"Are you telling me the whole story about your brother?"

"What do you mean?"

"Aren't you surprised by what he's doing? I know you said he's a drug addict, but there are plenty of addicts that aren't murders, let alone of their own families."

"You're right Sam, I didn't tell you the whole story. Michael isn't just an addict, he also has severe psychological problems. It started when he was sixteen and hurt his back in a motorcycle accident. He became addicted to Vicodin and couldn't shake it. Then as time went on, he got into cocaine and finally heroin. He was so high all the time, it affected his mind. My parents put him in several addiction programs, but nothing worked; that's why they disowned him. My dad hoped the threat of losing his inheritance would scare him and he'd straighten up, but it didn't work. The addiction was too strong and he always went back to drugs."

"Why do you think he waited until now to come back and kidnap Margret?"

"He must have found out that our mother had died and figured with her out of the picture he could force me to give him what he thinks is rightfully his. But you can see he's nothing more than a sick, degenerate killer who doesn't care about his family and never has. He must have taken Margret because Tommy told him she ran around with so many degenerates the police would never be able to figure out who did it if anything went wrong."

"Well, it looks like he's going to get his inheritance now. Is there any way to get around needing your sister's signature?"

"The bank president was my dad's best friend and the executor of my parent's estate, so I might be able to get him to help us. I'll go to the bank first thing in the morning and talk to him."

"If it's okay with you, I need to take a shower and get some sleep, I'm beat."

"Of course. I'll see you in the morning."

As I walked out of the room, Mary stopped me.

"Sam," she said, as I looked back, "tell me the truth. Given what my brother did to Tommy, do you really believe we'll get Margret back alive?"

While I was sure he wasn't going to leave anyone alive after he got the money, I decided it was best to keep that information to myself.

"Absolutely," I said, giving her a reassuring smile.

"God, I hope you're right. Goodnight."

"Good-night," I said, as I headed to the guest house.

That night I had a hard time sleeping; I guess that's one of the side effects of a near death experience. I thought about my dad and wanted to tell him that while he was right about a private investigator being a good fucker's job, there was a lot to be said for being a live fuckee.

The next morning Mary came to breakfast carrying a briefcase.

"The bank opens at nine, so I want to be there when Norman gets in."

"What are you going to tell him so he doesn't get suspicious and call the police?".

"I'll have to trust him and tell him the truth. He's like a second father to us, so I'm sure if he understands that Margret's life is in danger, he'll keep it to himself."

"Then I'll stay here and wait for your brother's call," I said as I walked her to the front door. "Good luck," I said, as she left the house.

As she was getting in the limo, Robert stopped her.

"Mary, you have a call on the house phone, it's Mr. Jenkins."

Mary followed Robert back into the house and he handed her the phone. Before she said anything, she covered the receiver and looked at me.

"What do you think he wants?"

"Probably just wants to know what's happening with Margret. Don't tell him anything."

"Hello, Charles … no, we still haven't heard from her … I know, I appreciate that … yes, I'll keep you posted. Goodbye."

"You were right," she said as she hung up the phone. "He was just concerned about Margret. Well, I've got to go. And, Sam, when Michael calls, you tell him that he doesn't get a cent of the ransom until we're sure Margret is alive and unharmed."

"I'll give him the message," I replied as I watched her walk out of the house and get into the limo.

CHAPTER EIGHT

WILL THE REAL KIDNAPPER PLEASE STAND UP OR AT LEAST RAISE YOUR HAND

As soon as Mary was gone, I decided to look in the father's study again to see if I could find a hidden picture of the brother. There was something about him killing Tommy and being willing to kill his own sister, that just didn't add up, no matter how psychologically fucked up he was. And if I knew what he looked like, I'd be able to verify he was the kidnapper. Since Robert was busy doing whatever he did when the sisters weren't around, like watching reruns of *The Nanny* or reading the latest issue of *Play Butler*, he wasn't paying attention to me, so

I went back to the study and started to look around. While I understood Mary's dad was disappointed and didn't want to be reminded of his son, but he was still his father, and a father never turns his back on his son. I knew that because when I left the agency and went off on my own my dad never turned his back on me; he just tore up a few of my baby pictures.

After looking through the study again, and only finding more pictures of everybody but the brother, I decided to go upstairs and check Mary's and Margret's bedrooms. If one of them was keeping a picture of their brother, it was more than likely there. As I walked into Mary's bedroom, the unmistakable smell of woman hit me, and I stopped and took a deep breath. The last time I could remember the smell of a woman's bedroom was before my divorce. But after my wife and my friend started screwing around, and she insisted we sleep in separate bedrooms so she could cheat without me knowing, the only smell I remember was the smell of deceit—that and Old Spice.

Now there was no mistaking that I was in a woman's bedroom. From the sweet scent of her perfume, to the stuffed animals she had on her bed, it not only reminded me of Mary, it also made me a little horny. I looked through her nightstand and chest of drawers, and besides spending a little too much time investigating her panties, I didn't find anything. But as I was about to leave her bedroom and move on to Margret's, I decided to check out her walk-in closet.

I know what you're thinking, but believe me I didn't do anything weird with any of her clothes, except for a little black cocktail number that was too tight on me. I was looking for that secret hiding place that all women have where they keep their intimate and private things; like dildos, diaries, and personal photos. That place where no one, especially a man, would ever think to look; my ex-wife's spot was under the covers on her side of the bed. The closet was as big as my apartment and stuffed with clothes, handbags, and at least a million pairs of shoes, and no, none of them fit me.

Since I learned through the years that most women hide their important things in either a purse or an empty shoebox, places a man would never touch, I opened every handbag and shoebox and didn't find anything. As I was about to give up, I happened to move a pile of sweaters on one of the closet shelves and saw a small wall safe.

"Here we go," I said as I started to rotate the tumbler on the safe to figure out the combination.

Thanks to a friend of my dads', who was a full-time locksmith and part time safe cracker for the local mob, I learned two important things as I was growing up, how to crack a safe, and mix cement.

"Safes are like women," 'Uncle Vito' would say, "if you want them to crack, you have to turn their knobs gently and listen for the clicks."

As I got older, I realized that while Vito was right about safes, he was wrong about women because no matter how gently I turned their knobs, I couldn't get into their cracks. Anyway, since Mary's safe wasn't very professional, I got it open in just a couple of minutes. But while the safe was cheap, the contents wasn't. I pulled out several very expensive pieces of jewelry and a lot of cash. There was so much expensive stuff, I had to make sure I was still in Mary's house and not Fort Knox.

As I inspected everything more closely, I kept thinking, *if I was a crook, I could retire with just this one heist*, but since I'm not, besides rubbing the cash against my body, I didn't take anything. As I was about to put everything back and move on to Margret's room, I saw a black book in the back of the safe that looked like either a diary or a small photo album.

"Bingo," I said, as I pulled it out and opened it.

It was another photo album containing more pictures of Mary, Margret, and their parents at various ages and occasions through the years. As I looked through the pictures, I was confused. Why would Mary keep a photo album hidden in a safe? Then suddenly I got my answer.

On the last page of the album, there was a picture of a blonde-haired, blue-eyed man in his thirties, sitting in a wheelchair in front of UCLA Medical Center in Los Angeles. I turned the picture over, and saw an inscription that read, "Michael, February 2016."

While the inscription verified the man in the picture's name was Michael and probably Mary's brother, it raised a lot more questions than it answered. Like, since the kidnapper had black hair and black eyes, and didn't look anything like the man in the picture, who was he? And why did Mary say she hadn't spoken to or seen her brother in several years, considering the picture proved she just saw him a few months ago? And what was he doing at UCLA? Since he was supposed to be in jail?

As I finished putting everything back in the safe, I thought about my next move. Since I couldn't tell Mary that I broke into her safe and found the picture of her brother, I had to get her to give me a description of him, so I could compare him to the kidnapper.

CHAPTER NINE

GIVE ME ONE MORE NIGHT, JUST ONE MORE NIGHT

As I walked out of Mary's bedroom, daydreaming about all the cash I had in my hands and against my body a few minutes before, I literally walked into Robert.

"Pardon me, Sam," he said, giving me a suspicious look.

Since I didn't want Robert to say anything to Mary about me being in her room, I had to use my well-developed investigator instincts and come up with an excuse. You're probably asking yourself what the difference is between a lie and excuse? Nothing, that's why my instincts are so well developed.

"Oh, Robert, I'm glad to see you," I said, smiling. "I was

looking for a bathroom and walked into this room by mistake."

Robert paused for a moment, processing what I said, then smiled, "Yes, sir, it's at the end of the hall on your right."

"Thank you," I said, returning the smile. "This place is so big and has so many doors, you need a map," I said, jokingly.

Robert smiled and walked away, and I continued down the hall and went into the bathroom, just in case he got suspicious and followed me.

After I finished in the bathroom, it turned out I did need to use it after all, and walked down the stairs to the living room, Mary came back from the bank.

"What happened? Were you able to get the money?"

"Yes, Norman was so upset about Margret, he agreed to help us. So he's allowing me to get the money with just my signature."

"That's great."

"Yeah, but there's another problem."

"What's that?"

"He needs another day to get that much cash together. Did you hear from my brother?"

The second she asked the question, I remembered needing her to give me the brother's description."

"No, but it should be anytime now."

"Do you think he'll believe us about the bank needing more time?"

"If he wants the money, he'll have to. Listen, Mary, since your father destroyed all the pictures of your brother, can you just tell me what he looks like, so I'll know."

The question obviously caught her off guard and she paused, "Ah, sure, Sam, he's thirty-five, tall and slim with black hair and black eyes."

"Black-hair and black eyes? That's odd, since everybody

else in the family is blonde with blue eyes," I said, suspiciously.

Mary paused for a moment before she answered, obviously thinking.

"He was blonde with blue eyes when he was living at home, but when he was disowned, he dyed his hair and started wearing black contacts, so he wouldn't have any family resemblance."

Based on the picture of her brother, her explanation sounded fishy. But before I could question her more, my cell phone rang.

"It's the kidnapper," I said as I looked at the incoming number and answered the call.

"Hello … yeah, this is Razor … yes, we can get the money, but we want proof that Margret's okay before you get it … your words aren't good enough, we want to see her for ourselves … that's fine, just text me the room number … and one more thing, the bank can't pull that much cash together by tomorrow, they need another day … Because it's ten million, not ten dollars … fine, I'll be there in fifteen minutes." I hung up the call.

"What's going on?"

"He's going to give us another day to get the money, and he's agreed to let me see Margret. I'm supposed to meet him at the Best Western on Russell, just off the 215."

"I'm coming with you."

"No, he wants me to come alone."

"Why? She's my sister."

"He probably wants to keep you and Margret separated, so he doesn't have any trouble."

"But I have a right to see my sister."

"You're right, you do, but trust me it's better this way. Besides, you need to stay here and make sure there are no problems with the bank. Don't worry, I'll make sure she's okay."

CARLO ARMENISE

"Okay, if you think it's the best way."

"I do. I'll be back as soon as I can," I said as I got the text and left the house.

As Alex drove me to the motel, I kept thinking about Mary's story about her brother changing his hair and eye color. The kidnapper I saw didn't look anything like the brother, and it was more than just the color of his hair and eyes. I knew that once I made sure Margret was okay, I had to follow up with UCLA, and find out about the Michael in the photo. As I planned my meeting with the kidnapper, I decided I had a couple of options.

First, I could just try talking him into releasing Margret, but considering I'd already tried using the talking approach with him, and it almost cost me my lips, I decided that option wasn't going to work. Or second, I could use force and just take Margret away from him. And even though I thought I could take him in a fight, that option was still risky, considering he had my gun and I didn't. So, I decided to wait until I saw Margret, and go from there.

When we got to the motel, I told Alex if I wasn't back in a half hour, to call Mary and have her call the police.

"You sure this is a good idea, Sam?" Alex said, as I got out of the car.

"It's all I got," I replied as I walked into the motel.

As I entered the motel lobby, the kidnapper, still wearing gloves, came up behind me and discreetly shoved a gun in my back.

"Keep walking and don't say a word," he said as he escorted me to one of the rooms on the first floor and knocked on the door.

A moment later, Diane opened the door.

"Get inside," he said as he pushed me into the room, shut the door and locked it. "Put your hands on your head," he said as he patted me down. "Now sit on the bed."

As I sat down on the bed, I tried to reestablish my connection with his girlfriend.

"Hello, Diane, it's good to see you again. How are you?"

She didn't answer; and if she did have something to say, the fresh bruises on her face showed the consequences if she did.

"Wait in the bathroom," he said to Diane.

"Get on your stomach and put your hands behind your back," he said as he took out a roll of duct tape from a duffle bag and taped my hands behind my back.

"Where's Margret?" I asked as he sat me up.

"She's in the bathroom. Diane, bring Margret out," he said, knocking on the door.

A moment later the bathroom door opened, and Diane lead Margret, who was blindfolded and gagged with duct tape, out of the bathroom and sat her in a chair near the bed. I could tell she was the real Margret by her crooked nose, and considering she looked like she slept in her clothes and hadn't showered in a few days, she was still sexy.

"You don't know me," I said to her, "but my name is Sam Razor and I'm a private investigator your sister hired to help bring you home. Are you okay?"

She paused for a moment, and then mumbled something through the tape. Even though I couldn't make out what she was trying to say, it seemed like it was something about the kidnapper.

"That's enough small talk, Razor. Now that you know she's alive, go back to Mary and tell her, for Margret's sake, the money better be ready the day after tomorrow. Take her back in the bathroom," he said to Diane.

As Margret stood up, she pulled away from Diane and threw herself on the bed next to me, mumbling frantically.

"Get her back in the bathroom," he said to Diane, as he pulled Margret up from the bed and pushed her back in the bathroom.

"It's time to go, Sam," he said as he took the duct tape off my hands.

As he finished removing the tape, I decided the physical force option was all I had if I wanted to rescue Margret. Realizing that I would be risking my life, a combination of fear and adrenaline surged through my body and I broke out in a cold sweat. Or maybe it was all fear and I pissed my pants again. Whichever it was, I knew I had to use the element of surprise and attack him when he wasn't expecting it. So as the last piece of tape came off my hands, I took a deep breath, kicked him in the chest and knocked him against the wall. Then I got up from the bed, pulled the gun out of his hand and hit him in the head with it. As he fell to the floor, I pointed the gun at him.

"Don't move," I said.

Under the circumstances, other than my heart beating so hard it felt like I swallowed a midget conga player, I felt proud of myself. I mean, I had conquered my fears and took care of business, now I just had to get Margret and take her home.

"Now get up slowly and keep your hands on your head," I said, as I kept the gun pointed at him.

"You surprise me, Sam," he said as he stood up and put his hands on his head. "All this time I thought you were weak."

"Whatever. Just tell Diane to bring Margret out."

"I'm afraid I can't do that," he said, as he lowered his arms.

"What are you doing? I'll shoot you," I said, as I cocked the trigger.

"I believe you," he said, smiling. "But not with that gun. It's your's and it's not loaded," he said as he walked toward me.

I might have fallen for the "gun's not loaded routine" when I was just starting out in the business, but I was a seasoned professional, and he'd have come up with something better than that.

"Well, let's just find out," I said as I pointed the gun at his leg and pulled the trigger. The gun didn't fire.

I pulled the trigger again and it still didn't fire. He was right, I did fall for the "gun's not loaded routine," because the gun wasn't loaded. Then he reached behind his back, took out another gun and pointed it at me.

"But this one is," he said, as he fired and hit me in the shoulder.

The pain from the bullet going into my shoulder was excruciating, and as the blood ran down my arm, I got dizzy and almost passed out. Holy shit! I thought, I'm going to die, right here in a single room at the Best Western. It could have at least happened at the Four Seasons, in a suite with cable and a minibar. As I got weaker, I sat down on the bed.

"I had a feeling you might try something heroic," he said, keeping his gun pointed at me and picking mine up from the floor, "so I had a back-up plan just in case. See, while I thought you were weak, I knew you weren't a coward. I don't know why I just don't kill you and get you out of my hair, but then I'd have to deal directly with Mary, and I don't want to do that. Now get the fuck out of here and wait for my call," he said as he pulled me up from the bed and pushed me toward the door. "And, Sam, if you try anymore heroics, the next time I'll aim for your balls," he said, pushing me out of the room.

CHAPTER TEN

A STITCH IN TIME,
TO STOP THE BLEEDING

After I left the motel, I had Alex take me to the hospital emergency room to get my shoulder looked at. As it turned out, I got lucky and the bullet had passed through my shoulder without causing any internal damage. So, after they stitched me up and gave me my allotment of pain pills and cherry flavored lollipops, I had Alex take me back to Mary's. On the way, I couldn't stop thinking about how the kidnapper outsmarted me. There was no way he was a psychologically impaired drug addict, and if he was, then I wanted to find a drug dealer as soon as possible. We got back to the house and Mary met me at the door.

"Oh my God, Sam. Are you okay?" she said, looking at my bandaged shoulder.

"It's just a flesh wound, a little gift from your brother."

"What happened?"

"I tried to rescue your sister, and it backfired."

"Is Margret alright?"

"She's fine. He had her gagged and blindfolded so she couldn't talk to me. Did you confirm the bank will have the ransom money the day after tomorrow?"

"Yes, it'll be ready first thing that morning. Why don't you go lie down and get some rest?"

I did need some sleep, but I also needed to go to UCLA.

"Since I can't do anything until the money's ready, I made an appointment with a specialist friend of mine in L.A. to look at my shoulder and give me a second opinion," I said, grabbing my shoulder and wincing in pain.

"I've got a great doctor here, Sam, if you want to have it looked at right away."

"Thanks, but I'd rather see my own doctor. I booked myself on a flight tonight and I'll come back tomorrow after my appointment."

"That's fine, Sam, you do whatever you need to do," she said as she moved close to me. "I can't tell you how much I appreciate what you've gone through for my sister," she said as she took my hand, looked me in the eyes, and gave me a kiss.

Suddenly, I forgot all about my shoulder and needing to go to L.A. I just wanted to stay here and let her show me more appreciation, if you know what I mean. But Mary was a client and I still had a job to do, so I left.

On the plane ride back to L.A., I kept fantasizing about kissing Mary again. It had been so long since I kissed a woman, I almost forgot how. So, to make sure I was ready the next time, I put my head down and practiced kissing the back of my hand.

It worked pretty good, too, until an overweight flight attendant saw me, smiled and winked. That's when I knew I'd practiced enough and was ready, for Mary that is.

Being close to death made me think about and miss my family, so I decided to go and see my mother while I was in L.A. I would have wanted to see Pepe, too, but I knew he'd just make fun of me for getting shot and want the money I owed him, which I still didn't have. While bloodstains and bandages will get you sympathy, preferred seating, and an extra bag of peanuts on airplanes, if I went to UCLA like this, they'd probably admit me. So, the first thing I did when I landed, was go to my apartment to take a shower, change clothes, and check on Shut the Fuck Up, who was still talking. Compared to Mary's mansion, my studio apartment felt like a broom closet and my claustrophobia kicked in. So after I put on my Pedro Armani suit, I headed for UCLA.

UCLA is in the heart of an upscale section of West Los Angeles, and is home to expensive shops and snobby restaurants that cater to the rich and famous. So if you don't have a lot of dinero, and I don't mean Robert, you should stay away from that area of town. Since I was injured, I decided to park in a handicapped space in front of the hospital. I know you're thinking that only an asshole would take up a parking space needed by a real handicapped person, and you're right, but what's your point?

Anyway, as I walked into the medical center, I decided the best place to get the information I wanted about Michael was the admissions desk. Like most people, hospitals give me the creeps. It seems like every time I visit someone, I get sick. I think it's psychological. You're in a place where people are sick and your mind tells you to join them. Whatever it is,

I wanted to get in and out of there as soon as possible. As I walked up to the admissions desk, I approached an older female hospital volunteer.

"Can I help you?" she asked.

"Yes, I'm looking for a patient named Michael Whitfield," I said, giving her a big smile.

"Are you a family member?" she asked, sternly.

I knew if I wanted to get her to give me information about Michael, I needed to turn on the charm.

"Yes, sweetheart," I said, winking at her, "I'm his brother and I just got back from a tour in Afghanistan. I heard he was in the hospital and wanted to surprise him."

Hearing the word "sweetheart" she smiled again and started to soften.

"Afghanistan, huh? Are you in the military?"

"Yeah, honey. the Army."

"Well, thank you for your service," she said, licking her lips seductively. "Let's see," she said, as she checked her computer, "what did you say your brother's name was again?"

"Michael Whitfield."

"I don't see anybody by that name registered in the hospital. Are you sure he's at UCLA?"

"Positive. Maybe you missed him," I said, as I tried to see the computer screen.

"Sir," she said as her demeanor changed and she gave me an annoyed look, "I am a trained hospital volunteer and we don't misplace patients."

"Sorry, darling," I said, turning on the charm again. "Is that a list of just current patients?"

"I thought you said he was a current patient?" she asked.

"That's what my mother said, but maybe he was released,

and she forgot to tell me. Where would I get information on released patients, honey?"

"The administration office on the third floor," she said, smiling again.

"Thank you, you've been very helpful. And by the way, you're doing a great job," I said as I winked at her and walked up the stairs to the third floor.

As I got to the administrative office, I decided that if I encountered another trained, older female volunteer, I'd have to turn on the charm thick from the beginning. Even though, until that point in my life, I never had a problem schmoozing old women. They were usually attracted to me like kids to a carnival. It was the younger ones that usually gave me the cold shoulder. Anyway, at least now I knew Michael wasn't currently at UCLA, which meant the brother could be the kidnapper with dyed hair and black eyes, but was he? As I walked into the administrative office, all I saw was older female volunteers, so I picked out one who looked like a cross between Phyllis Diller and Woody Allen.

"Excuse me," I said, giving her a seductive smile.

"Can I help you, sir?" she said.

"Yes, you can, but first has anyone ever told you, you look just like Sophia Loren?"

"No," she said smiling. "Do you really think so?" she said as she batted her eye lashes flirtatiously.

"Absolutely, but you're better looking."

"Thank you," she said as she put her hand on mine. "And you're pretty cute yourself."

Like kids to a carnival, I thought as I looked at her name badge and smiled.

"Stella, that's a beautiful name."

"Why thank you," she said as she squeezed my hand. "Now how can I help you, handsome?"

"I'm trying to track down an Army buddy of mine that was a patient here. Can you tell me when he was discharged?"

"What's his name?"

"Michael Whitfield."

"Let's see," she said as she smiled seductively and checked the records. "Here we are, Michael Whitfield. He was here, but I'm sorry to tell you he passed away from cancer a few months ago."

"Oh my God!" I said, pretending to be shocked, "I can't believe it. He was healthy as a horse. Do you happen to know the address of his family, so I can send my condolences?"

"It says his body was released to his sister, a Mary Whitfield in Las Vegas.

"Thank you, Sophia, I mean, Stella. I can't tell you how helpful you've been.

"It was my pleasure," she said, grabbing my hand again. "I get off in an hour, if you need a little comforting."

"That's a great offer, but I'll have to take a raincheck. I need to talk to my friend's family, and I'm afraid I wouldn't be able to tear myself away if we got started. Goodbye."

"Good-bye. I work every Tuesday, if you change your mind and want to have lunch sometime," she said as she smiled again and winked at me."

"I'll call you," I said as I winked back at her and walked out of the office.

CHAPTER ELEVEN

THE TRUTH SHALL SET YOU FREE, THAT AND A LOADED 45

The trip to UCLA taught me a few things. First, that Mary's brother was the guy in the picture and not the kidnapper I met, unless he came back from the dead. And second, that Mary was deliberately not telling me the truth about her relationship with her brother, and about him being in jail. It also told me she knew who the real kidnapper was, and why he kidnapped her sister. Now I needed to know why she lied to me and put my life in danger. That was another chapter in the P.I. Manual that I obviously didn't study well enough. It was the one on not believing everything your clients say and letting it cloud your judgment. It was true.

Throughout my career I heard all kinds of bizarre stories

from spouses justifying their cheating, like my ex-wife for instance, and I was always able to tell when they were bullshitting. But in Mary's case, I dropped my guard and let my feelings for her get in the way. Like I said, I had a feeling the story about her bother was a lie, but I trusted her and didn't press her on it. But now I needed the real story, before I had to deliver the money.

After I left UCLA, I headed back to my apartment to change clothes again and feed Shut the Fuck Up, who was still talking. On the way, I popped a few more pain pills, ate a couple more lollipops, and tried to keep my fake designer suit from getting wrinkled; that was hard to do, since Pedro's suits were perma-wrinkle to begin with. I decided not to visit my mother because I knew she'd see my shoulder and want me to stay in L.A. so she could take care of me; DNA remember? So instead, I jumped on the next flight back to Vegas.

I got back to Mary's around four o'clock and found her in the backfield taking a swim. As I walked up, she saw me and got out of the pool wearing a skimpy black bikini.

"Sam, when did you get back?" she asked, wrapping herself in a towel and sitting in a deck chair.

I was glad she covered up, because the sight of her in that tiny bikini made it hard to concentrate. It was so small, I had to use my imagination to figure out what was left to my imagination.

"I just arrived," I said, sitting in a chair next to her.

"What did your doctor say about your shoulder?"

"He, ah, confirmed it was just a flesh wound and that I should be good as new in a month or so."

"That's great news. Did my brother call to tell you where to take the ransom tomorrow?"

"No, not yet. Will the bank have the money ready?" I asked getting ready to confront her about what I knew.

"Yes. I'll pick it up in the morning."

"That's good," I said as I leaned in close to her, "but it's too bad your brother will never get it."

"What do you mean?" she asked, concerned.

"He won't get it, because he's dead. Your brother, Michael Whitfield, who you supposedly haven't heard from in years and was in jail, died of cancer a couple months ago at UCLA. But you knew that, because you buried him here in Vegas."

"How did you find out?" She asked, shocked that I knew.

"I did some investigation; that's what I do for a living remember? So, why don't you cut the bullshit and tell me the truth, about everything."

She paused for a moment, then took a deep breath.

"Okay. You're right, my brother is dead, he died of brain cancer. I did lie about that, but I didn't lie about him being a drug addict and being disowned. I also lied about not having seen or spoken to him. When my mother found out he was sick and told me, I reached out to him to offer my support and help him financially. I was also the one who got him into UCLA for treatment, but I didn't tell the rest of my family because they wouldn't have approved. But I couldn't just stand by and watch him die alone," she said as she started to cry.

Seeing how distressed she was, I momentarily felt sorry for her and handed her a Kleenex I had in my pocket.

"Thank you."

"You lied about more than that," I said, restraining my sympathy. "You know who the real kidnapper is, don't you?"

"Yes. His name is Jimmy Hallon and he's an ex-con that

worked as an orderly at UCLA when my brother was there. I met him a few times on my visits to see Michael. He found out that we had a lot of money, and after Michael died, he decided he was going to get some of it and planned the kidnapping."

"How did the Broker get involved?"

"Michael asked me how Margret was doing, and I told him that she was dating a mobster named Tommy "The Broker" and he must have told Jimmy. Then Jimmy found out about Tommy's money problems, and told him if he helped with the kidnapping, he'd get some of the ransom."

"That didn't work out so well for Tommy. So Margret doesn't know anything about Jimmy?"

"No, she doesn't know about Jimmy or Michael dying. As far as she knows, Michael and Tommy are the kidnappers."

"And that's why Jimmy keeps her blindfolded, so she won't know he's not her brother," I said as that puzzle piece fell into place.

"So you see, Sam, I couldn't tell you the truth, because I didn't know what Jimmy would do to Margret if I didn't go along."

For the first time, it felt like Mary was finally telling me the truth about everything and I believed her. But there was still one question I needed answered.

"So, if you knew about Jimmy and were planning to give him the money all along, why hire a private investigator?"

"To make it look like I was helping Margret without getting the police involved. And to act as a go-between and deliver the money, so it looked like I didn't know what was going on."

"But why me?"

"You were recommended by a former client of yours, an ex-con friend of Jimmy's. He said you wouldn't figure out what was going on and cause trouble."

"You mean, dumb?"

"Let's say inexperienced when it came to a handling a kidnapping case. You were just supposed to deliver the ransom and bring my sister home. That was it. We didn't plan on you following Tommy and meeting Jimmy, or figuring out he wasn't my brother. But as it turned out, you were a lot smarter than we thought and now your life is in danger. Can you forgive me?"

Forgiveness. I heard that word a lot in my line of work, especially from the person caught cheating. And while her lies put my life in danger, it was still better than sitting in my car, tracking another cheater, so I smiled and took her hand.

"I forgive you," I said, smiling. "But no more lies, deal?"

"Deal," she said as she leaned in and gave me another kiss. Which, because of practicing on my hand, I did really well.

CHAPTER TWELVE

WOULD YOU LIKE CHEESE WITH THAT CASH?

Anyway, now that I knew the real story about Jimmy, I needed to come up with a plan for delivering the money that had a chance of keeping Margret, Mary, and me alive. Jimmy called at eight o'clock that night, and instructed me to put the money in two large suitcases and bring it and Mary to the house where he killed Tommy by eleven the next morning. I knew why he wanted the money in suitcases, and why he wanted Mary to be with me, but I had other ideas.

"He wants the money put in two large suitcases and for you to come with me to deliver them."

"Why?"

I didn't want to tell her, because if I was right, it would mean we'd all end up dead, but since we made the deal not to lie to each other, I told her the truth.

"He plans to kill us after he gets the money," I said, as tactfully as I could.

"Oh my God! Do you really think so?"

"Yeah. He can't risk leaving anyone alive and turning him in, but don't worry, I have a plan of my own. I'll tell you about it while we're packing up the money."

The next morning Mary picked up the money from the bank, bought two large suitcases and came back to the house. I'd never seen that much money in my life. And as we were putting it in the suitcases, I must admit I was tempted to misplace a little of it in my pockets, but I didn't; and I'm not lying.

After the cash was ready, I decided to take a cab to the house instead of having Alex take me and risk his life, too. So, at nine-thirty the cab showed up, and wouldn't you know it, it was the same Pakistani cab driver I had the last time I went to the house. But this time, instead of his old, beat-up cab, he was driving a new, big-ass Mercedes, compliments of the fare I paid him.

We loaded the suitcases in the trunk of the Mercedes and, with Mary standing in the driveway wishing me good luck, I left for the house. Good luck. People say that because it's supposed to cancel out the possibility of having bad luck, but under the circumstances, bad luck seemed more likely. On the way to the house, I prayed the exchange would come off without a hitch and we'd all end up alive; don't forget, praying is part of my Italian/Mexican Catholic DNA. My plan was simple. I had Mary stay at home, out of harm's way, and wait to hear from me after the exchange was over and Margret was safely on her way back to the house. We got to the house at five minutes to eleven, and I had the driver park up the street like before.

"Keep the engine running like you did before," I said normally, knowing he spoke better English than I did, "and I'll be back as soon as I can."

"Be safe, my friend," he said, smiling as I got out of the cab. "And don't worry, the meter will be running, too."

"Thank you," I said, knowing he was smiling because he was thinking about the next Mercedes he was going to buy with the fare I'd be paying.

I took the suitcases out of the trunk and hid them behind a large bush in front of the house next door, then walked to the front door. As I was about to knock, the door opened and Jimmy pulled me into the house and held a gun to my head.

"Where's Mary and the money?"

"She's not coming and the money's hidden outside."

"Go get it."

"No, not yet."

"What the fuck game are you playing, Sam?" he said, as he cocked the trigger on the gun and pointed it at my balls, "Don't forget what I said I would do if you tried anymore fucking heroics."

"Don't worry, you'll get your money," I said covering my balls with my hands, "but not until Margret is safe. Or does that screw up your plans to kill us all, Jimmy Hallon?"

When he heard me say his real name, he looked concerned. "Did Mary tell you?"

"No, as it turned out, I wasn't as dumb as you thought, and figured it out for myself. I just want to know if you planned the kidnapping before Michael died, or did you have a hand in that, too?"

"He was dying anyway. I just put him out of his misery.

Now, what do you want, Sam?" he asked as he moved the barrel of the gun back up to my head.

"I want you to let Margret go. And when I'm sure she's safely on her way to Mary, I'll give you the money. Then you can keep me as a hostage until you get away. But if you do anything stupid, like not letting Margret go or killing me, you won't get the money and Mary will go to the cops."

"How do I know she won't go to the cops anyway after I let Margret go?"

"She won't, as long as she knows I'm safe after you get away. So, have we got a deal?"

He paused for a moment, thinking and then opened the basement door.

"Diane, bring Margret upstairs."

A moment later, Diane brought Margret, still blindfolded with her mouth and hands duct taped, up from the basement.

"Margret, it's Sam Razor, are you okay?"

She nodded yes and mumbled something.

"What's going on, Michael? Where's Margret's sister and the money?

"You can cut the Michael crap, Diane, he knows who I really am."

"He does? I didn't tell him, Jimmy, I swear," she said, fearfully.

"Just shut up and take the duct tape off her."

"Why?"

"We're going to let her go."

"What? Why?"

"Because we don't get the money unless we do. Now stop asking fucking questions and take off the duct tape."

"And the blindfold, too," I said.

"No, the blindfold stays on until she's out of the house."

As soon as the duck tape was off Margret's hands and mouth, she pulled off the blindfold.

"You assholes," she screamed, and pushed Diane into Jimmy.

Diane and Jimmy fell against the kitchen wall, and Jimmy lost his balance. As he tried to regain it, Margret kicked him in the balls and he dropped his gun and doubled over in pain on the floor. I picked up the gun and pointed at him.

"You think it's loaded this time, Sam?" he said, as he stood up.

"How about I find out?" I said, as I moved the barrel down to his balls and cocked the trigger.

"That's okay," he said, knowing the gun was loaded.

"Now both of you get on your stomachs on the floor."

After Jimmy and Diane got on the floor, and I tied their hands behind their backs with a couple of kitchen towels, I walked over to Margret.

"Pulling off the blindfold was a gutsy thing to do."

"Well, I'd rather be killed then let this slimeball, pretending to be my brother, get away with the money."

"So, you knew all along he wasn't your brother?"

"My brother's dead. Besides, Michael would have never done anything like this."

"I'll call your sister and let her know you're safe and Jimmy didn't get the money," I said, as I took out my cell phone. "And then I'll call the police," I said, looking at Jimmy and Diane.

"Where's the money, Sam?" Margret asked.

"I hid it behind a big bush in front of the house next door. It's in two suitcases."

"While you're talking to Mary, I'll get it and bring it inside so no one will steal it," she said as she walked out of the house.

Since I hadn't charged my cell phone in a while, when I tried to make the call to Mary, the phone was dead. So, while

I waited for Margret to come back in the house, I turned my attention back to Jimmy and Diane.

"Stand up and put your backs against the wall."

As they got up from floor, Diane looked at Jimmy.

"I can't believe we got outsmarted by this dumb-ass," she said, pointing at me.

When she called me a dumb-ass, I got pissed off. I mean she was the one going to jail and I was the dumb-ass?

"Don't worry," Jimmy said to Diane, "it's not over."

"Don't listen to him, Diane, it's over," I said, with a tone of satisfaction. "And like I said, you're both going to jail for a long time."

At that moment, Margret walked back into the house carrying the two suitcases and set them down.

"No, they're not," she said, as she pointed a gun at me. "Drop your gun, Sam, and untie them."

"What's going on, Margret?" I said, dropping my gun on the floor and untying Jimmy and Diane.

"What does it look like?" Jimmy said, as he picked up the gun and pointed it at me again. "Margret and I are partners."

I must admit I didn't see this coming. Margret and Jimmy partners in a kidnapping scheme? But why? Margret already had all the money she could use, and Jimmy was a degenerate killer. But since there wasn't a chapter in the P.I. Manual on how to get out of a situation like this, all I could do was stand there with my thumb up my ass.

"What do you mean, Jimmy?" Diane said, getting angry. "Are you and this rich bitch together?"

"Who are you calling a bitch? You stupid cunt," Margret said.

This was good. If the two women got into a hair pulling, knock down brawl, that ended in a sexy pillow fight, and distracted Jimmy enough so I could jump him and get his gun, it would be perfect. But unfortunately Jimmy didn't have the same pillow fight fantasy I did, and he stopped the fight.

"That's enough, you two. Look. Diane, me and Margret are together and have been for a while."

"But you said you loved me, Jimmy," Diane said as she started to cry.

"Love you?" he said laughing, "I was just using you."

"You fucker," she screamed, as she took a knife off a kitchen counter and ran toward him. "I'll kill you."

Before she could stab him, Jimmy shot her in the stomach and she slumped to the floor.

Man, since I started this case one person already got killed, and two people got wounded, myself included, so I hoped I wouldn't end up being the second person in the kill column. But knowing Margret and Jimmy were on the same side and had both the guns, I knew my chances of getting away alive were slim and none, and slim was standing over with them. So I decided the only thing I could do was try and talk my way out of it.

"Why are you doing this, Margret? You've got plenty of money already."

"Not without Mary I don't. That's why I planned my own kidnapping, to get the money without Mary's approval."

"That's enough talk, Razor, you don't need to know anything else. Let's go down and join your dead friend, Jimmy, in the basement."

"Wait a minute," I said, as he opened the basement door, "don't forget Mary knows where I am and if I don't call her, she'll go to the cops."

"No, she won't," replied Margret. "While I was outside, I called her and told her we were safe and that I already called the police to come and get Jimmy. I also told her to stay at the house until we got there. By the time she realizes were not coming, we'll be long gone with the money."

Another chapter of the P.I. Manual I knew I would use eventually, was the one on how to shift the focus of suspicion away from yourself and back to the suspect. And considering the danger I was in, it was time to use it.

"Did Jimmy tell you he killed Tommy?" I asked Margret.

"Yeah, but he said it was self-defense."

"That's enough, Sam, get down in the basement," he said, trying to push me through the door,

"Did he tell you he also killed your brother," I yelled out.

While the information about Tommy didn't get a reaction from her, the Michael information did.

"What's he talking about, Jimmy?"

"Don't listen to him, your brother died of brain cancer, you know that," replied Jimmy.

"But you told me you helped put him out of his misery," I said, to raise her suspicions even more.

"Is that true, Jimmy?"

"Don't let this fuck get in your head, Margret, we have to go."

"Is it true?" she said, angrily.

"Look, you know how sick your brother was, and that it was only a matter of time before he died."

"Oh my God!" she screamed. "You murdered my brother," she said, as she pointed her gun at Jimmy and cocked the trigger.

"What are you doing, Margret, put the gun down," Jimmy said.

"I can't believe what I've done," she said as she started to cry, "I helped kill my own brother."

"Just put the gun down, baby. Once I get rid of Sam, there

won't be anybody left to ruin our plan."

"No, you're not killing anyone else," she said. "Drop your gun."

"What are you going to do, turn yourself in? Remember, the kidnapping was your idea."

"That's right, but I'd rather take my chances with the police then let you hurt anymore innocent people. Now drop your fucking gun," she said, as she fired and hit him in the shoulder.

"You crazy bitch," he yelled as he dropped his gun and grabbed his shoulder.

"I'm sorry, Sam, I didn't mean to put you in danger," she said as she kept the gun pointed at Jimmy."

"You can tell me your story later," I said as I rubbed my own shoulder and picked up Jimmy's gun. "Now this time, call the police for real while I tie Jimmy up."

As Margret started to make the call, and I started to tie Jimmy's hands behind his back, the front door opened, and Jenkins walked in escorting Mary, and holding a gun.

"I don't think so," he said. "Now both of you drop your guns."

Margret and I dropped our guns, and Margret looked at Mary.

"I'm so sorry," she said tearfully.

"What are you doing here, Charles?" Jimmy asked, as he walked over and picked up Margret's gun. "We were supposed to meet at your office once I had the money."

"Let's just say I wanted to come and protect my investment," replied Jenkins.

I didn't see this coming either. This case had more twists and turns than an Italian/Mexican wedding, and there was nothing in the manual that could have prepared me for it.

"Mary, are you, all right?" I asked.

"I'm fine, and you?"

Before I could answer her, Jenkins pointed the barrel of

his gun at her head.

"She's fine," said Jenkins. "Just a little surprised to find out her sister was behind her own kidnapping."

"Why, Margret? Why did you do this?" Mary asked.

"For reasons you wouldn't understand," Margret replied.

"As touching as this reunion is," said Jimmy, "it's time to end it. Now everybody, get down to the basement."

"Not so fast," Jenkins said, as he pushed Mary aside, pointed his gun at Jimmy and picked up one of the suitcases. "We need to talk about my split of the money first. I've decided it's gone up to five million."

"What the fuck are you talking about?" Jimmy said, as he pointed his gun at Jenkins. "We agreed you'd get two million. The million Margret owes you, plus a million for keeping your mouth shut about the kidnapping."

"You owe Charles a million dollars, Margret?" Mary questioned.

"That's right," said Jenkins. "Your sister has a serious gambling problem and I hold quite a few of her markers. And under the circumstances," he said to Jimmy, "I've decided my cut is fifty percent."

Just when I thought I couldn't be surprised by anything else, this new fact about Margret's gambling debt threw me for a loop.

"You can't double-cross me like that," Jimmy said to Jenkins.

"Now, Jimmy, don't think of it as a double-cross, think of it as a bonus for me saving your ass," replied Jenkins.

"You're right," replied Jimmy as he suddenly grabbed Margret and held his gun to her head. "It looks like we've got what you call a "Mexican stand off," said Jimmy, smiling.

When Jimmy said that, it really pissed me off. There was no such thing as a Mexican stand off, my mother's side of the family always shot first.

"You've got a sister and so do I," Jimmy said, pulling Margret closer to him, "but mine is the one that owes you money. So, if she dies, and you get caught, you lose it all."

"Okay, you win," said Jenkins. "I'll take the two million like we agreed."

"No," said Jimmy, "considering you tried to fuck me over, your share has dropped back to a million."

"Whatever you say," replied Jenkins.

"That's smart," Jimmy said, keeping his gun on Jenkins and pushing me toward the basement door. "Now let's get rid of all the witnesses."

"Lead the way," replied Jenkins, grabbing Mary and pushing her toward the door, while he continued to keep his gun aimed at Jimmy.

Jimmy took Margret and stepped in front of Jenkins and Mary, and pushed me through the door. Knowing Mary, Margret, and I were all going to die if I didn't do something, I gave Mary a look that indicated for her to follow my lead.

"Now," I yelled as I pushed Margret into Jimmy causing him to let go of her and fall back. At the same time, Mary pulled away from Jenkins and grabbed his gun hand. Jenkins' gun accidentally fired and hit Jimmy in the leg, and Jimmy fired back, and hit Jenkins in the stomach. As Jimmy grabbed his leg and lost his balance, I grabbed his gun hand and we started to wrestle.

As I threw him to the floor, the gun went off again and shot me in the side. Driven again by self-preservation and another rush of adrenaline, I ignored the pain and continued to wrestle for the gun. As I was about to get the gun out of his hand, he rolled on top of me and pointed it at my head.

"I should have killed you when I killed Tommy," he said, as he prepared to pull the trigger.

At that moment, the front door flew open and the hooker from the casino, dressed in a police uniform, ran in followed by several other uniformed officers, all carrying guns.

"Police!" She yelled. "Drop your gun," she said to Jimmy.

But instead of dropping his gun, Jimmy fired at her and missed. She returned fire and hit him in the chest. As he rolled off me onto the floor, she walked over.

"Are you all right, handsome?"

"Never better," I said, as I saw the blood flowing out of the bullet hole in my side and passed out.

CHAPTER THIRTEEN

ALL'S WELL THAT ENDS WITH JUST A FEW BULLET WOUNDS

The next day I woke up in the hospital with tubes coming and going from my body and machines on both sides of my hospital bed beeping and whizzing and displaying all kinds of different numbers. I think hospitals put these machines in your room to make you think they're doing something they can justify charging you a fortune for.

As I wiped the sleep from my eyes, I saw that I was covered in so many bandages I felt like I should be able to speak Egyptian. As I tried to move, the pain in my side from the most recent bullet wound was so strong I almost started to cry. I said almost, because big Italian/Mexican men don't cry, they just whine a lot, which is also in our DNA. I saw that I had a button attached to one of my hands, which I figured was either a nurse's call button or something for the pain if I needed it. And boy did I need it. So I pressed the button, hoping it wasn't just a call button, and immediately felt a sense of euphoria and calm come over my body as the pain went away. *Wow*, I thought, *it was morphine.*

At that moment, because of how great the morphine made me feel, I decided if I healed too fast, I'd shoot myself in my other side so I could use it again. As I tried to sit up, the door to my room opened and Mary walked in.

"Good morning," she said, as she walked over and stood next to my bed. "How are you feeling?"

"Never better," I replied, smiling, and this time I really meant it, as I pressed the morphine button a couple more times. "How long have I been here?"

"A couple of days. The doctor says you're doing great and should be ready to leave tomorrow."

Hearing what she said, I wondered if Amazon sold a portable morphine machine.

"How's your sister?"

"She's being held in county jail until the arraignment. I just came from seeing her and she wanted me to tell you how sorry she is for what happened to you."

"I still don't understand why she did it."

"She didn't think she had a choice. Charles threatened her, and she thought if she told me about it, I would have just ridiculed her for making bad decisions, and refused to help her. Unfortunately, that's how I've treated her in the past when she made mistakes. And after Jimmy led her to believe the kidnapping would get her the money she needed to pay her gambling debt, she felt like it was her only choice. You want to know the saddest part of all this?"

"What?" I said, as I pressed the morphine button again to keep from getting too sad.

"I was so focused on my brother and helping him, I didn't realize my sister needed my help, too."

"What's going to happen to her?"

"We don't know. Our attorney thinks she'll do some jail time for being an accessory, but since I'm not pressing charges and she didn't have anything to do with Tommy or Michael's murder, it shouldn't be too long. I hope."

"For your sake, I hope so, too."

"Thank you again for everything you did, Sam. In fact, I have something for you," she said, as she took an envelope out of her purse and handed it to me."

"What's this?"

"Open it."

Considering all the bandages they had me in, I couldn't manipulate my hands, so I handed it back to her. "You'll have to do it."

She opened the envelope and took out a check for fifty thousand dollars and showed it to me.

"What's this?"

"It's the bonus you earned for finding my sister and saving her life."

"But I didn't stop the kidnapping."

"Sure, you did. And more importantly you saved me and my sister's relationship, and that's worth more to me than anything else," she said as she leaned over and gave me another kiss.

I couldn't believe it. I got a check for fifty grand and another kiss from Mary. I felt so good, I didn't need any more morphine, but I took some anyway just in case the feeling didn't last. As I looked at the check again, the door opened again and a woman dressed in a police uniform walked in.

"Hey handsome, how are you feeling?" she said as she walked over to the bed. "Remember me?"

At first, I couldn't figure out who she was, then it came to me, it was the hooker cop.

"Sure I do, you're the hooker, I mean, police officer that saved my life."

"My real name is Detective Jean Simmons. I was working undercover as a hooker at the Crystal Palace to watch Jenkins. We've had him under surveillance for several months for fraud and embezzlement and thanks to you, we were able to put him and Jimmy behind bars for a long time."

"I only have a question?"

"Sure," she said.

"How did you know to come to the house when you did?"

"Your Pakistani cab driver called us."

"No shit. I'll bet he kept his meter running," I said laughing, and taking another hit of morphine.

CPSIA information can be obtained
at www.ICGtesting.com
Printed in the USA
BVHW04s0016060718
520775BV00031B/267/P